# A Recipe for Murder

*Jeffrey Ashford*

# A RECIPE FOR MURDER

WALKER AND COMPANY
NEW YORK

First published in the United States of America
in 1980 by the Walker Publishing Company, Inc.

ISBN: 0-8027-5423-6

Library of Congress Catalog Card Number: 80-51721

Printed in the United States of America

10   9   8   7   6   5   4   3   2   1

# A Recipe for Murder

# 1

The rain was heavy and the north-east wind was driving it against the window with a slashing, drumming sound: the edge of the lawn was almost under water. It was more like mid-November than mid-September.

Detective Sergeant Kelly said: 'Proper weather for ducks.' He had a round, plumpish face whose underlying expression was one of relaxed contentment. It was easy to judge that not much rattled him.

Scott crossed to a wall switch and started the fan blower. Heat began to spread through the small, beamed room. 'Grab a seat. And how about a cup of coffee?'

When Kelly said he'd like one – 'Can't ever resist a coffee' – Scott went through to the kitchen and switched on the electric kettle. He collected together mugs, milk, sugar, and instant coffee. The kettle boiled and he put water in the mugs and added coffee. It took time to find a tray because Avis was not the tidiest of housewives, but having found it he carried the coffee through to the sitting-room.

'It's certainly not the weather for farming,' said Kelly.

'If you listen to any farmer, no weather ever is.'

'You don't farm, then?'

'I write.'

'D'you mean, you write books?'

'Yes.'

'My missus'll be tickled pink to hear I've met you: tremendous reader, she is. What name do you write under?'

'My own.' He was cynically amused to note from Kelly's expression that he'd obviously never even seen a book by Kevin Scott.

'I'm sure she'll have read and liked your books,' said Kelly manfully. 'The trouble for me is, I don't get much time for pleasure reading.'

'These days, not enough people do . . . Help yourself to milk and sugar.'

Kelly leaned forward until he was sitting on the edge of the chair. He put three spoonfuls of sugar in one of the mugs. 'I've always had a sweet tooth. When I was a nipper I used to stand in front of the farthing tray of sweets and wonder which offered the best value . . . It's a long time since there were trays of farthing sweets.'

Scott waited for the further observation that the world had changed a lot, but this didn't come. Kelly added milk, then picked up the mug and sat back. A spring twanged loudly, startling him.

'It always does that. We bought the suite at a sale for twelve pounds and it's been ringing the changes ever since.' Scott offered a pack of cigarettes.

'Thanks. The missus is always on at me to give up smoking, but – ' He came forward, balancing the mug in his right hand, and took a cigarette from the pack. When he settled back, the spring twanged again. 'Sounds a bit like loose change to me.'

Scott smiled.

Kelly rested the mug on his right knee. 'As I said, we've had this report. I hope you'll understand, Mr Scott, that it doesn't matter how crazy a report, we have to check on it.'

6

'So what crazy report has brought you here?'

'We've been told that your wife's missing and something must have happened to her.'

'Who in the hell's been wasting your time with that nonsense?'

'A Miss Holloway. Apparently Mrs Scott was due to ring her in London, but didn't, and this so worried her that she repeatedly rang this house without getting an answer.'

'And that was enough to make her get on to you with that crazy allegation? She's even more mentally unstable than I thought.'

'Your wife is perfectly all right?'

'Of course.'

'Is she here now, in this house?'

'No, she isn't.'

'When did you last actually see her?'

'I went up to London on Tuesday and she drove me to the station.'

'When did you return from London?'

'Wednesday afternoon.'

'And she didn't meet you at the station – weren't you expecting her to?'

'Yes, but she wasn't there so I caught a taxi.'

'Surely you were worried by her absence?'

'No.'

Kelly chose his words carefully. 'But if your wife had made all the arrangements – '

'She's an independent person who often pursues her independence fairly vigorously.' Scott's tone was ironic. 'When she wasn't at the station, I assumed she'd decided on the spur of the moment to go and stay with friends and had just forgotten about meeting me.'

'But . . .' Kelly clearly found difficulty in envisaging

7

a wife who could act like that. 'But in that case, surely you've rung friends to check where she's staying and that she's all right?'

'No. I respect independence.'

Kelly, still bewildered, changed the conversation. 'I presume Miss Holloway is a close friend of your wife?'

'That is how she'd describe the relationship.'

'I heard that she was almost hysterical when she telephoned.'

'She is hysterical both by nature and choice.'

'You sound as if you don't like her?'

Scott didn't answer.

Kelly rubbed his square, blunt chin. 'Rightly or wrongly, she is very worried that something has happened to your wife.' He hesitated, then said rather diffidently: 'Mr Scott, would you describe your marriage as a normally happy one?'

'Are you suggesting that the normal marriage is happy?'

'I'm asking you about yours.'

'I was brought up only to discuss other people's marriages, never my own.'

Kelly sighed. 'I think the best thing I can do is leave you my telephone number.' He took a card from his battered wallet and put this down on the occasional table by his side. 'When you know for certain where your wife's staying, perhaps you'd give me a ring?' He stood. 'Sorry to have interrupted your writing: I hope it hasn't upset the inspiration.' He walked across to the panelled wooden door, reached for the thong which lifted the broad latch but then checked his action. He turned back. 'There is one more thing. Do you know a Mrs Ballentyne?'

'How's that of the slightest consequence?'

'Miss Holloway said that you and the lady were friends?'

'Quite right. But friends in the old fashioned, pre-permissive-age sense.'

'Yes, of course. Please don't forget to phone, then, as soon as you've had word from your wife.' He pulled open the door of the sitting-room and went into the hall and Scott followed him. As he stared through one of the windows, he said for the second time: 'Just the weather for ducks.'

# 2

After a wet, miserable June, July had finally introduced summer to the countryside. Much of the sunshine seemed to fade for Scott when he went downstairs and saw the parcel on the porch seat, left there by the postman an hour earlier: he could be certain that this was his script, sent to the publishers five weeks before. Of course, they might merely be returning it for minor alterations . . .

He went along the hall to the kitchen, where he plugged in the electric kettle to boil and then made two mugs of coffee.

Avis was sitting up in bed, reading a women's magazine. She was looking provocatively lovely. Her blonde, naturally curly hair was in some disorder yet it artfully framed her oval face: her peaches-and-cream complexion needed no make-up: her deep blue eyes, set above a classically shaped nose were, without any deliberation on her part, looking slightly soulful: her full lips, so promising in shape, were moist and slightly apart: her nightdress was filmy and the outlines of her shapely breasts were visible. Oh well, he thought, as he put one mug down on her bedside table, he wasn't the first man to have made a fool of himself over a beautiful woman.

She looked up. 'D'you know what I've just read?' Her voice was low and a shade husky. 'In the fur sales in London, Marquans offered a ten thousand pound Russian sable coat for three thousand. I've always wanted a sable coat.'

He wondered if there were anything expensive which she had not, at one time or another, coveted.

'I ran into Maureen the other day when I was in Fishers. She couldn't wait to tell me that Joe has bought her a new fur coat.'

'Sable?'

'Ranch mink.'

'Tightwad.'

She frowned. 'Why do you always sneer about everybody?'

'Sheer envy.' He didn't really envy Joe one little bit, but his major defence to an unhappy marriage was an ironic amusement of life's absurdities.

'If you'd get a proper job and make some money you wouldn't be so eaten up by envy.' She'd said the same thing too often to sound truly resentful now. 'When we were engaged and just after we were married we used to go out and have fun, but you won't go anywhere now.'

A man's engagement should never be held against him: innocence was so often naive.

'When did we last go out to a dance? Not since the midsummer ball, and I only got you to that after a hell of a struggle. Yet Joe takes Maureen out at least once a week. They're off to the Grand to-morrow. She asked me why didn't we make up a party?'

'I trust you explained the facts of life as related to expense accounts?'

'I keep telling you, I'll pay.'

'Thanks, but we'll wait until I can afford to take you.'

'You're riddled with ridiculous pride.'

Could one have pride in one's lack of success?

'God, how I hate living here, in this grotty place.'

The clapboard cottage was two hundred years old.

11

It had beamed ceilings, low lintels, ingle-nook fire-places, a hall which had been an outshut, and some of the original plaster made with cow dung. He loved it because it was quiet time passed.

'What is so terrible is that you've got a good brain. If only you'd chuck up writing and get a job you could earn a decent salary and we wouldn't have to live like paupers.'

He suddenly needed to explain, deliberately forgetting all the previous times he'd tried. He wrote, despite his lack of financial success, because he had faith in himself as a writer. Every time he sat and typed 'Chapter One', he was certain that now he was going to write the book which would win recognition from the critics and the public. Then, as chapter followed chapter, he sadly became aware there had been a communications breakdown between mind and fingers and that although this book would (hopefully) be published, it would not be the knife to life he had intended. It was this which so frustrated and depressed him. Yet he 'knew' that with the next book the miracle would happen and intention and performance would become one. That was why he had to go on writing.

She said petulantly: 'I just don't understand the point of going on and on when you don't make as much as a garbage collector.'

He should have saved his breath for cooling the coffee. He drank, to discover that the coffee had become cool without the effort.

She put her empty mug down, climbed out of bed and stretched. 'I think I'll go up to London for the day. I haven't been around the shops in ages.' She crossed to the cupboard, which was built to the side of the huge central chimney which came up from downstairs, opened the door, and stared at her many dresses. She chose one and put it on the bed, pulled her nightdress up and over her head. She smiled with satisfaction when she saw the expression on his face. He thought, as he left the bedroom, that God had overarmed the female sex when He gave them both a tongue and a body.

He went downstairs and put the mugs in the kitchen, returned to the hall and unlocked the porch door. He picked up the parcel and two letters with it: both the letters were for Avis.

Back in the kitchen he used a sharp knife to open the parcel. There was a folder and inside that his script and a letter.

The editor, a charming man in his late fifties, possessed endless, at times repetitious tact. Two readers had read the script and unfortunately their reports had been somewhat critical. He himself had read it and was forced to agree with their criticisms. Knowing what a perfectionist Kevin was, he was certain Kevin would not wish the script to be published in its present form. Kevin, of course, might be tempted to submit the script elsewhere, but he did most sincerely (underlined) hope that Kevin would accept the verdict and put the script to one side and not bring an end to a collaboration which had led to several very good books being published.

Scott swore.

.        .        .        .        .

It was the following Tuesday, cloudy but with sunshine forecast for the afternoon, when Avis looked across the breakfast table and said: 'Shouldn't you be hearing from the publishers about your latest script?'

If an element of the unexpected helped keep a

13

marriage from becoming stale, then his should have been as fresh as the proverbial daisy: there were many times when Avis totally surprised him. He would have said she was far too uninterested in his work to have the slightest idea when he'd sent the script off. He buttered a second piece of toast. 'As a matter of fact, I heard from them the other day.'

'Did they like it?'

'Along the lines of the curate's egg.'

'What's that mean?'

'Charles admired my punctuation. Unfortunately, he was less enthusiastic about the opening, the way the plot developed, the characterisation, and the ending.'

'Are you saying he's rejected it?'

'But in style, as one would expect from Charles. Pass the marmalade, will you, please.'

Her voice rose. 'Is that all you've got to say – pass the marmalade? What are we going to live on now? My money, I suppose?'

'I've never asked you for a penny towards house-keeping and I'm not starting now.'

'You're great on declarations. The integrity of the writer. The distance between art and money. But you'd soon start moaning if I didn't keep on buying extra food which you can't afford.'

'I could probably survive without brie and smoked salmon.'

'You eat them quickly enough when they're on the table.'

'I'm far too afraid of pain to cut off my nose to spite my face.'

'Always the smart answer. If you're so clever, why in the hell don't you write a smart book and make some money for a change?'

14

It was a good question.

She suddenly stood up. 'I just can't take the atmosphere any more. You're always the same when something goes wrong with your writing. I'll stay with someone for a couple of days until you've got over it.'

'Who's the someone – Fiona?'

'What if she is? She's been my friend from way back and I'm not going to stop seeing her just because you don't like her. And if we're going to start criticising each other's friends, what about yours?'

'What about them?'

'Don't think I don't know about Jane.'

He looked astonished, then laughed. 'With your imagination and my punctuation, we ought to be able to write a book that even Charles would really like.'

She hurried out of the room. He heard her feet clack across the tiled kitchen and hall floors. The stairs creaked one after the other, as they always did. She went into their bedroom. Her footsteps were muffled when she was on the carpet, hard and sharp when she moved off this onto the floorboards.

The logical thing to do was to cry quits, divorce, and put the five years down to experience. Writers were supposed to be ready to pay heavily for experience. But he'd been blessed with parents who'd lived by outdated precepts. They had believed in duty. When a man gave his word, he stuck to it through thick and thin. (Small wonder that in the last ten years of their lives they had found the world a very odd place.) They had taught him to believe in duty and this was why he would never divorce Avis, though should she divorce him he would accept her decision with relief.

# 3

Avis's mother, a woman of very decided opinions, had succinctly explained the facts of life. 'They're all the same, even your father: only one thought in their heads. And don't you ever forget – beforehand its orchids, afterwards it's dandelions.'

Her parents had been wealthy. They'd lived in a large house, set in a garden of over two acres which had been landscaped by Mills. At a time when very few people employed even a single servant, they had employed a married couple as butler and cook, a full-time parlourmaid, and a chauffeur/gardener: in addition, on four days a week a woman had come up from the village to do the more menial housework. Before going to finishing-school in Yverdon, Avis had never cooked, washed-up, made a bed, darned a sock, or sewn on a button. At the finishing-school, as a preparation for Life, she had been taught to cook mignon de bœuf en croûte.

Frank had proposed to her, but his parents had been rather coarse. Jonathan had proposed to her, but he was the second son and as her mother had so wisely said, a second son came into neither the title nor the property. Peter had been going to propose to her, but after a while something must have happened because he'd seen less and less of her and in the end had become engaged to a woman of doubtful social status. And then she'd met Kevin and after three weeks and two days he'd proposed to her and she had accepted . . . If only her parents hadn't been in that road

16

smash which had left them both invalids, unwilling to bother about anybody but themselves. If only, after their deaths within six months of each other, it hadn't turned out that they'd been living on capital and over-drafts so that instead of leaving her a fortune, her father, the last to die, had left her a bare thirty thousand pounds . . .

Through the windscreen of the Jaguar, Avis saw the call-box and braked. There was a lay-by road, serving a row of shops, and she drew into this to park behind a van which was unloading. She opened her handbag and brought out a slim gold cigarette case and picked out a cigarette: she snapped open a gold lighter. Did she really mean to make the phone call? she asked herself, a little frightened but also, to her surprise, more than a little excited.

When Kevin had proposed to her, he'd bemused her with tales of success. She'd seen herself as the wife of an internationally acclaimed author, hostess to the famous. Reality? A small, cramped, mean little cottage, no help, hardly ever going out, never going abroad, unknown to the famous. 'Before it's orchids, afterwards it's dandelions.'

So now she was going to pick those orchids for herself.

She left the car and dropped the cigarette on to the pavement, unaware that since lighting it she had not once smoked it. She went into the call-box, placed some money ready, and dialled.

A woman, her voice thick with the local burr, said: 'Who is it?'

'I want to speak to Mr Powell.'

' 'Ang on.'

There was a short wait before a man said: 'Powell speaking.'

'You sound as if you're a bit huffy to-day.'

'Are you sure you've got the right number?'

'Now don't get pompous. I told you the first time we met, I can't stand a man becoming pompous.'

His tone changed. 'Where was that? At the mid-summer ball?'

'No clues.'

'We danced three dances together.'

'Did we?' She remembered the way his hand had fondled her back even during the first of those three dances and how he'd smiled when she'd demanded he stop it, as if he had sensed her mood of discontent. 'The most eager lecher of them all,' her mother had once said, 'is the man of fifty who's beginning to wonder how much longer he'll be active and is desperate to convince himself it'll be a long, long time.'

.     .     .     .     .

It was three weeks later, on the third of August, when Avis telephoned Fiona Holloway. 'Look, love, will you do me a favour?'

'Of course I will,' Fiona answered eagerly.

'Cover if Kevin rings and tries to get hold of me: I don't suppose he will, but just in case. I've told him I'm spending to-night with you.'

'Where will you be if I do need to get hold of you?'

'That would be telling!' Then, with intentional cruelty, she added: 'I'll do the same for you some day.' As if Fiona could ever need that kind of help!

'When are you coming up, Avis? It's simply ages since you've been . . .'

'I'm afraid I've been terribly busy. But I will drop

in sometime and see you.' As she said goodbye and rang off, she imagined the hurt expression on Fiona's face; thick, heavy, her face was topped by hair of such a bright ginger shade that it looked as if it must be dyed, but wasn't. Jumbo, they'd called her at school, with all the callousness of the young.

Avis returned from the call-box to the Jaguar and drove off. If Kevin had been even half successful, then, instead of being on her way to the motel, the two of them could have been now driving down to Duen-sur-Mer, still largely unknown to most holiday-makers, still chic, where they had had their honey-moon. Life had been all champagne bubbles then.

.    .    .    .    .

The Red Barn Motel was midway between Fering-ton and Hemscross, on the lower Canterbury road. Twenty cabins, faced with unbarked wood, were set ten on either side of the double storey brick building which had originally been a public house. In this central building was the reception desk, a restaurant, and a bar.

Avis walked through to the reception desk. 'You've a cabin booked for me. Mrs Smith.'

'That's right, Mrs Smith.' The receptionist wondered why people never stopped working the Smith, Jones, and Brown routine. His gaze wandered down her body.

Normally, she would have met his visual lechery with cold disdain, but now it added an extra dimension of excitement. She smiled at him.

'Number ten cabin. That's the end one to the right, as you go out of the door. If you'll just sign the register.' He swivelled a heavy ledger round on the

19

counter. 'Would you be kind enough to pay the twelve pounds fifty now, please.'

She drove the Jaguar the hundred yards to the end cabin and backed it into the garage in one lock – she was a competent driver. She picked up her small suitcase and went through the inside doorway into the very small lobby, off which led the bedroom and bathroom.

In the bedroom there were two single beds, two wooden chairs, two bedside carpets, two bedside tables on one of which was a phone and on the other some plastic flowers and a 'Notices to Guests', and a gorblimy dressing table.

She placed the suitcase on one of the beds, lifted the lid, brought out the bottle of whisky which lay on top of the clothes and carried this over to the dressing table on which was a plastic tray with mugs and a water container. She poured out a strong whisky and added only a little water. Normally abstemious, excitement was urging her to drink heavily.

She raised the glass in a toast. To the second Mrs Julian Powell.

.        .        .        .        .

Powell's father had been a farm labourer who never knew what it was like to enjoy security: he lived all his married life in tied cottages and his wages were never quite enough to meet the family's expenses. He died, arms lacerated by a cutter which he had tried to clear without switching off the power, two years before he would have retired on a pension that would have given him at least the illusion of security. Powell's mother had been a small, faded woman who had been meek and mild in most things, but who would fight the devil himself if the needs of the family demanded this. She had had four children, three boys and one girl. Tim stayed on the land, a solid, dependable labourer like his father. Reginald drifted to the towns and, rootless, became mixed-up with the outer criminal circles. Maude went behind the Dutch barns with various lads, became pregnant, and married. But Albert, denying his heritage became rich.

He'd been eight when he'd gone with his father to the home farm of a large estate. The owners had been away and they'd been taken by the head cowman to see the main house from the outside. The house had overwhelmed Bert. He'd no idea that any building could be so huge. Then, as he'd continued to stare at the south face, he had experienced a growing and urgent belief, incredible in view of his background, that one day he would own such a house and estate. Being eight, he'd promptly told the two men this. His father, a man of great understanding, had listened gravely, but the head cowman had jeered at such nonsense. 'The only way you'll ever get to live inside a house like that will be as a pissy-weak indoor servant.'

But for the fact that his mother had always been of an unyielding moral character, it might have been supposed that Bert's father had not been Powell. The rest of the family were not bright, but he was sharply intelligent; where they drifted with life, not knowing or caring where they were going, he fought life, determined to wrest from it all he wanted: where they met failure with resignation, he met it with curses and increased resolution.

At eighteen, after two years of night school, he

gained a scholarship to an agricultural college and changed his first name from Albert to Julian. By twenty-seven he was assistant farm manager to the Lastey estate in Shropshire, five thousand acres of rich farm land which bordered the Severn. Most men would have been proud of attaining such a position, but ambition left him discontented even when it became clear that the farm manager would be retiring soon and there was every chance of his being offered that position. Even as farm manager, he would be a very long way from being the wealthy landowner he was determined to become. How to grab hold of the next rung of the ladder and climb?

Judith Duffield was too tall, her shoulders too broad, her features were plain and heavy and unless she was very careful her upper lip bore the beginnings of a moustache. But her father had left her sixteen thousand pounds, when that was quite a large sum of money.

Fifteen thousand pounds was the asking price for Shufflewood Farm: four hundred and fifty acres of once rich farmland which had been allowed to run right down, five large outbuildings in need of repair, a couple of worn-out tractors and some equipment, and a herd of thirty cows which were said to be Ayrshires, but whose mothers had obviously wandered.

Judith, four years older than Powell, had received several proposals from men who had decided that beauty wasn't everything, but Powell was the first who persuaded her that he really needed her for herself. The strength of his cause had lain in the fact that he genuinely and desperately did need her because Shufflewood Farm was a bargain.

During their fifteen years at Shufflewood Farm she learned, at first with bitterness, then with resignation,

22

that need and love were not synonymous: he learned, with a growing sense of resentment, that she was nobody's fool. She wouldn't sign the farm over to him. What he never had the wit to realise was that beneath those unfortunate looks was an infinite capacity for affection and had he ever shown her real love she would have happily signed over to him everything she owned.

At the end of those fifteen years the nearby town had doubled in size and Shufflewood Farm now lay on its northern outskirts. A property developer offered half a million pounds for the farm and then raised this to three-quarters of a million when the competition began to grow. The Powells sold.

Tregarth House, in the parish of Finchstreet, was set in a park of twenty-five acres. Beyond the park was the home farm of seven hundred acres and a further fifteen hundred acres of woodland. The deeds were made out in Judith's name, despite all his efforts to have her agree to their being in their joint names.

Tregarth House was Edwardian, built on the site of an Elizabethan manor. Architecturally it was unremarkable, aesthetically it was clumsy and even absurd, not least because of the crenelated and pillared entrance porch, There were three floors and a wing, containing twenty-three bedrooms (fourteen of these were on the top floor, small, cramped, and for the servants), six bathrooms, a billiards room, two sitting-rooms, a dining-room, a breakfast room, a library . . .

Powell liked to stand on the small balcony leading off the upstairs sitting-room and remember how, when he had been eight, that head cowman had said that only as a pissy-weak indoor servant would he ever live in a big house. Now the house, fields, and woods were his (which is how he saw them). Beyond,

23

six miles to the south, was the sea: sometimes he even felt as if he were master of that as well.

.     .     .     .     .

Powell drove a Rover 3500: he liked comfort and prestige, but not ostentation except in the matter of land and beasts. At fifty-one he was hard-muscled and on many days he spent the same hours in the fields as his men. His face mainly suggested strength: rugged, chunky feature were overlaid by wiry hair, only now faintly tinged with grey: his brown eyes held steady and his chin was pugnaciously square: only his mouth betrayed his one weakness, a driving lust equal to that of any of his prize Romney Marsh rams.

On the journey to the Red Barn Motel his imagination was stretched with the pictures of the pleasures to come.

# 4

For Steven Ballentyne, there had never been a to-morrow: life was to-day. He and Jane had had seven years of excitingly happy marriage and then he had died on a tennis court, just after a wild and hilariously missed smash. He left memories whose exact details might fade but whose colours could not, a large number of debts, and a widow who for many months had wanted to die.

She slowly picked up the pieces of her life. The large house had to be sold because she could not afford the mortgage repayments: the capital which remained after paying off the mortgage company covered all the other debts, but left only a few thousand pounds over and above them. She had trained as a secretary before marrying and so found little difficulty in getting a good job in Ferington, with a firm of local solicitors. She moved into a flat whose rent was more than she should have afforded, but from the sitting-room, six floors up, she could look over a forest of roofs to the green fields beyond the town.

She was attractive rather than beautiful, warm-natured rather than passionate. She was always neat, but never bothered as to whether she were dressed in fashion: she used a little make-up when she remembered to do so.

At six-thirty on Tuesday she carried the typed witness statement through to one of the partners' office.

'Thanks a lot for staying on,' Reynolds said. He looked at his watch. 'I'm afraid it's late and I shouldn't have asked you to complete it to-night, but we've got to get the papers to counsel as soon as humanly possible . . . How about having a drink as a thank-you?'

'No, thanks. As a matter of fact, I've a date a little later on.'

'Oh, well, some other time.'

She left. She collected her handbag from her room, put on a lightweight mackintosh to save carrying it, and went downstairs and out to the street.

Despite the extensive development Ferington had endured, Bank Street was still virtually as it had been thirty years before: the road of the Forty Thieves the old locals called it because along it were many of the town's solicitors', architects', and accountants', offices and three out of the four banks.

A soft wind came up the sloping road to flap the hem of her mackintosh against the backs of her legs. Suddenly, and for no readily discernible reason, she was reminded of Steven . . . Why did memories still suddenly rush in to harass her emotions and turn the world black? She ought, she decided, to have accepted Reynolds's offer of a drink: after all, he had never shown any of the traits of an office Romeo.

She walked up to the T-junction, to the left of which the road had been filled in to form a pedestrian precinct. She was hungry, yet for the moment she dreaded returning to the empty flat . . . Some of the shops had late night opening and a stationer was one of these. She went inside.

The books were in the middle of the shop. From the moment she could first read, she had turned to books for pleasure, interest, amusement, or comfort.

'Are you about to do some starving author a good turn and buy his book?'

She turned and smiled at Scott. 'I would if I could. But books cost so much these days that all I can do is look at them in the shops. There's one on costumes I thought I'd buy – until I saw the price.'

'How much – ten pounds?'

'Nineteen pounds ninety-five pence.'

'Ouch! But just think – at normal royalties that would be one ninety-five in the author's pocket.'

'Do you always think of books in terms of what they make the author?'

'What other way is there of looking at them?' He grinned. 'Don't tell me you believe in that awful tag, art for art's sake? Remember your Johnson.'

'Johnson was a horrible old cynic.'

'The perfect definition of a professional author.'

'I refuse to believe you write just for the money.'

'You think that there must be easier ways of starving?'

'I've read all your books.'

'That's probably a unique claim.'

'One day you're going to write something important.'

'Now how do I respond to that? I can't modestly deny everything you've just said because the inference is that all I've written to date is unimportant and I agree.'

'You always denigrate your own writing, don't you? Why? Is it really embarrassment? Your work isn't as good as you meant it to be and therefore you can't accept it's as good as it is?'

'I'm not prepared to answer questions like that without due notice . . . Look, are you in a hurry?'

'Would I be standing here, just chatting, if I were?'

'Good. Then come and have a coffee or a drink?'

She hesitated.

'I'm a grass widower for the night and I'm stuck on page forty-one and waiting for inspiration to strike. It often strikes when I'm having a drink with a friend.'

'All right. Let's go and await the coming.'

.    .    .    .    .

Avis picked up her glass and stood. 'Have another drink, Julian?'

'I don't want another drink, I want – ' began Powell.

'You've made that very obvious.' She laughed. She walked from the chair to the gorblimy dressing-table. In the mirror, she could see him, sitting on the bed. Red-faced, sweating, and very frustrated. She poured herself a large whisky.

'Why the hell – ' He stopped.

'Why the hell what?'

'Nothing.'

She added a little water to the whisky, returned to the chair.

He said loudly: 'Why d'you say to meet here if you weren't going to . . .' He stopped again. A man of crude passion, he suffered a strange inability to put that passion into words.

'I wonder why so few men ever learn to be subtle?' she remarked.

'What d'you mean, subtle?'

'To sit back and enjoy the travelling instead of always desperately rushing to arrive.'

She was a bitch, Powell thought bitterly. She'd led him on and then suddenly slammed the gate and laughed at his frustration. She didn't understand how a man could be overwhelmed by his needs. Years and years ago, Tim had said to him: 'I tell you, Bert,

28

it's like a bloody gut-ache that drives a bloke crazy.'
Was this desperate sensuality the one legacy left to
them by their father?

Unexpectedly, she came and sat on the bed by his
side. Immediately, he lost all sense of resentment and
knew only the violent need. He put his arm round her
and felt her snuggle up against him.

'You know, a woman likes to be able to believe
she's wanted for herself, not just for her body.'

He unbuttoned the top of her dress.

'Poor Judith!'

'Forget her.'

'Don't be so unchivalrous. She can't help being
who she is. But really you know, it is a pity she
doesn't learn to take more care over her appearance.'

He slid his hand inside her dress and she made no
move to resist him. This time, he thought triumph-
antly.

'And the jewellery she was wearing wasn't really
her. I mean, she needs something discreet. But that
rather ostentatious brooch . . . She was telling me
all about her collection of jade jewellery.'

His hand cupped velvety smooth flesh.

'She was quite pleased because some jeweller thinks
he may be able to get her a necklace in the shape of a
seahorse.'

He kissed her and tried to ease her back on to the
bed.

'D'you know, Julian, ever since I've been a little
girl I've wanted a jade seahorse.'

'For God's sake, lie back.'

She disengaged with skilful ease, stood, and
buttoned up her dress. 'An aunt of mine had one and
I wanted it so much I even asked her if she'd give it
to me. She wouldn't, of course. It's funny how one

often wants things desperately for no apparent reason.

'Avis, darling, please, you've got to – '

'Try travelling a little more slowly, Julian, and then maybe you'll arrive. Provided you remember.'

'Remember what?'

'To be subtle, of course,' she answered.

# 5

Scott disliked gardening and so when the Jaguar swept into the drive he dug the fork into the ground and straightened up, thankful to stop work.

As Avis rounded the house to come out of its shadow into the sun he thought how beautiful she was. If only her parents had taught her that money wasn't everything, that success didn't always smell sweet . . . Clichés? But what was 'If only' if not the biggest cliché of them all?

She went into the house without bothering to greet him. During their short engagement, he'd always humoured her out of her moods. If only he'd had the sense to realise that it would have been far better to . . . If only . . . Reluctantly, he returned to his digging.

Some twenty minutes later, Avis came out of the house and across the lawn, which needed cutting. 'I stopped at Linda's on my way back,' she said, her voice sharp. 'Caroline dropped in while I was there. She went shopping in Ferington on Tuesday evening.'

'Is that fact supposed to hold some special significance for me?'

'Are you trying to say you've forgotten where you were on Tuesday evening?'

'I'm afraid so.'

'You're a poor liar.'

That was correct. But his parents had so instilled in him the sharp difference between right and wrong that he'd never been able to convince himself he was doing right when he knew he was doing wrong. 'I apologise for my shortcomings.'

'Always the smart-alec answer.'

He sighed. It was a lovely evening, the kind of warm, still, late summer evening when peace rode the tree tops.

'You were in Ferington.'

'So what did I do in Ferington? Walk straight past Caroline without seeing her?'

'You didn't see her, but she saw you!'

He suddenly remembered. 'I suppose I was having a drink in the courtyard at the Wine Shop.'

'Far too engrossed to notice her.'

'Because I was enjoying a discussion on whether tragedy is an essential ingredient of comedy.'

'Do you really expect me to believe that?' Her voice became spiteful. 'I went up to London for the night and you couldn't wait to see your girl friend.'

'Jane is – '

'I know exactly what she is without you having to tell me.'

'You don't know anything. I met her in Broughton's, we had two drinks at the Wine Shop, and I walked her back to her flat. And to forestall the next accusation, no, I did not go up to her flat with her.'

'Liar!' she shouted and returned to the house.

He lit a cigarette. He wondered why, since he'd never given her cause for jealousy, she was now making such a fool of herself? It didn't occur to him that she could be suffering from a conscience and needed to justify herself to herself.

.    .    .    .    .

There were two doors at the north end of the down-

32

stairs sitting-room in Tregarth House, one of which led to the dining-room and the other to a built-in strong-room. Powell stared at the strong-room door. There was a sound from behind him and he whirled round to face Mrs French, the daily woman who apart from their housekeeper was the only help in the house.

'Is something wrong, Mr Powell?'

'Nothing,' he replied.

'It's just that you looked kind of funny.'

'A touch of indigestion.'

'You're like my Alf: been suffering from it something shocking these last few days. As I said to him – '

He abruptly cut short her meandering reminiscences and crossed to the far end of the sitting-room and the library.

He walked over to the large bow window, with deep oak frames and leaded panes, and stared out at the rolling fields, some down to grazing, some ready for harvesting. In the fifty-acre field, in one of the paddocks into which the field had been divided, the herd of two hundred and fifty milking Friesians, whose average milk yield was now the highest in the county, were grazing. For once he studied them without interest.

He turned and looked at the shelves of books which lined the walls. Judith had bought all Kevin Scott's books and professed to enjoy them. He found them unreadable. In his imagination he saw Avis, all inhibitions finally overcome, lying naked on a bed . . .

The grandmother clock in the sitting-room struck midday and as the last chime died away he heard a distant door slam shut. Mrs French had left, dead on time, as always. The housekeeper, Olive Bins, had the morning off and so now he was on his own.

33

Kevin had once told him – in that self-mocking way of his – that he worked office hours, so that it was probably Avis who would answer the call. He crossed to the phone on the desk to the right of the ugly fireplace.

She did answer. 'It's Julian. Look, I've got to see you again.'

'I think you must have the wrong number.'

He could visualise the mocking expression on her face. 'I can't give you that jade necklace, but I'll buy you something nicer . . .'

'You've obviously already forgotten what I told you about being subtle,' she cut in. 'If you have to try and buy your favours, at least don't make it too obvious.' She cut the connexion.

# 6

'Have you rung Barnes yet?' Judith asked, as she looked at her husband across the breakfast table.

'No.'

'He said it was important.'

'He can bloody wait.'

She looked more worried than resentful. 'What's the matter, Julian?' she asked quietly.

'Nothing.'

'There must be. You've been on edge for days. Mrs French said only yesterday that she thought you weren't well.'

A sudden gust of wind shook the window of the breakfast room, a long, narrow room beyond the dining-room.

'Are you sure you're feeling all right?' she persisted.

He was feeling lousy. But how could she begin to understand what ailed him when for her sex had always been one of those things, like going out to dinner, more duty than pleasure?

'Don't you think it would be an idea to ask Dr Redmayne to call and give you a check-up?'

'There's no need. For God's sake, stop flapping.'

She sighed. 'You're so stubborn. Well, I don't care what you say, if you're no better soon I'm asking Redmayne to come here.' She paused. 'I'm driving over to Madge's after I've cleared up. We're having a coffee morning to start a fund to buy a kidney machine for the younger boy of the McGarthys.'

She had an infinite capacity for worrying about the sick and the lame, he thought.

'Aren't you eating anything more?'

'I'm not hungry.'

Judith cleared the table, putting some things in the heavily carved oak sideboard and the rest on a tray. 'I'll be off as soon as I've stacked everything in the washing-up machine.'

She carried the tray out through the serving room. She would, he knew, have much preferred to live in a smaller house, not because that would have been much less work but because the trappings of wealth and privilege made her feel uneasy. That was why, as Avis had so cruelly pointed out to him, she could not wear any of her larger and more valuable pieces of jewellery without their appearing ostentatious . . .

Judith looked into the room and was obviously surprised to find him still there. 'Have you seen my handbag? There it is! I knew I'd put it down somewhere.' She entered and picked up the handbag from a chair. 'You won't forget to ring Barnes?'

'No.'

'Then I'm off.' She left.

He walked through into the sitting-room, lit a cigarette, and stared at the door of the strong-room. He'd gone to Werner and Hall three months before to look at some jade and they'd mentioned the possibility of their buying in the seahorse necklace. A week ago they'd phoned to say they now had it. He had not mentioned this to Judith . . .

It wouldn't be as if he were giving to Avis something which actually belonged to Judith.

.   .   .   .   .

Avis struck the Chinese gong in the hall. Scott, in the spare bedroom upstairs, flexed his fingers as he stared at the paper in the typewriter. He'd written several pages in the morning: more to the point, he'd managed to nail down the main characters from the beginning.

He left the bedroom, ducking under the lintel. Avis was in the dining-room, setting the table. 'The typewriter's been sounding like a machine-gun all morning. Have things been going really well?'

He was surprised at her interest. 'I'm at the stage where Dostoyevsky is relegated to the back seat: disillusionment shouldn't set in until chapter six.'

'Maybe this time it won't.'

'Let's keep fingers and toes crossed and pray to the patron saint of scribes. By the way, who was the phone call from earlier on – anyone important?'

'It was Susan, telling me about her new kitchen.'

'Totally unimportant.'

'Not if you're interested in how the cooking goes – which I hope you are since I've spent all morning making a steak and kidney pie and orange chocolate.'

'What's all this in aid of? I haven't missed out on an anniversary, have I?'

'There's no need to be so rude. Can't I cook you a special meal simply because I want to?'

'Whenever you feel the urge, succumb immediately.'

She laughed as she left to return to the kitchen.

Echoes of the past, he thought, with brief nostalgia. During their engagement and for the first few months of their marriage, they'd laughed a lot.

She brought in the pie, gravy, boiled potatoes, and peas. He cut through the crisp crust.

'You'd better have that piece and give me a much smaller one,' she said. 'I weighed myself on Maureen's scales yesterday and discovered I've put on four pounds.'

'Things are even more serious than you imagine. I'm reliably informed that she keeps her scales reading half a stone underweight so that she can convince herself she's not quite as fat as she looks.'

She giggled. 'I'll tell her that.'

'And bring a beautiful friendship to an abrupt end?'

'You and Maureen? That'll be the day!' She was silent until he'd served her then, as she helped herself to one potato and some peas, she said very casually: 'Did I mention Fiona?'

'Not for the past ten minutes.'

'She rang up when you were out in the garage. The poor thing's in a hell of a state.'

'That's nature's fault.'

'Show a bit of the charity you're always preaching . . . She's had a bad go of the flu and the doctor kept her on antibiotics for days and days and now she's feeling suicidal. She asked if I could go and cheer her up. You wouldn't mind if I nipped up for the night, would you?'

'Now I understand why we're eating like this.'

'For your nasty, suspicious mind, I'd decided on the meal yesterday and Fiona didn't ring until this morning.'

'Psychic premonition.'

If you'd any psychic premonition you wouldn't be smiling, she thought contemptuously. God, men were blind fools!


·       ·       ·       ·       ·


A different night clerk was behind the reception

38

desk at the Red Barn Motel. He was middle aged, dyspeptic, and far more interested in his slipped disc than in lascivious day-dreams.

Cabin ten was as impersonally neat as before. She put the small suitcase on one of the beds, opened it, and brought out a bottle of whisky which she placed on the gorblimy dressing-table. She knew both excitement and a sense of triumph and as soon as she had finished the first drink, she poured herself another.

.    .    .    .    .

Powell, conscious of the mocking expression on Avis's face, said uneasily: 'That necklace – you won't . . .' He stopped.

'What won't I do?'

'You won't wear it, will you?'

'Why not?'

'Well, it's just . . .' He stopped again.

'You are odd!' She rolled over and kissed him, making certain her breasts pressed hard against him.

He began to stroke her back, experiencing a fresh surge of lust although his violent passion was not long since satiated. 'Judith's going away for a couple of days very soon,' he said hoarsely.

'So?'

'So we can see each other for as long as we want.'

'Where are we going to meet?'

'What's wrong with here? It's handy.'

She began to move. When he tried to hold her to himself, she knocked his hand away and then swivelled round to sit on the edge of the bed. 'You're not worried at coming to this place?'

'Worried?' he repeated stupidly.

'It doesn't make you feel cheap and nasty?'

39

'Of course not.'

'Well, it does me.' She stood. 'I'll tell you exactly how it makes me feel. Like a tart.'

He stared at her body.

'I have to book in in a false name and then wait in this ghastly cabin until you sneak in. It's all so horribly sordid.'

'Then we'll go to one of the London hotels . . .'

'You think that will make a difference?' she asked scathingly. 'You don't begin to understand, do you?'

He didn't – not then.

She crossed to the nearer chair, on which were her clothes, and picked up the necklace. She ran her fingers along the beautifully carved seahorse.

'What d'you want, then?' he demanded.

She came up to the bed and when he reached out she did not this time move away. His hands cupped smooth, warm flesh and his needs became still more urgent.

'If Judith's going away . . .' She stopped.

'Lie down on the bed.'

'Why don't I come to your place?'

He had been about to kiss her flesh. With his mouth only an inch from her body, so that his breath warmed her, he said: 'What?'

'Why don't I move in with you?' She gathered his face up against herself. 'We'd be able to have all the fun in the world.'

'It's impossible,' he answered, his voice muffled.

'Why?'

'Olive's there.'

'You're not worried about her seeing me, are you?' She began to move her hips.

'You're talking crazily.'

She pushed him away. She opened the clasp of the

necklace and put the fine gold chain round her neck. She began to dress.

'We daren't use my place. Can't you understand that?'

'I understand precisely what you really think of me,' she replied coldly.

When his passions cooled, he began to understand what she really thought of him.

# 7

Because of her character, Judith had never once in the twenty-three years of their marriage challenged Powell with the fact that he had married her for her money. But she was a woman of stern rectitude. So if she discovered that he had betrayed her for a younger, beautiful woman, her reactions would not be mild and of the permissive age, but of an earlier, strait-laced era when the way of the transgressor was made harsh. Knowing his deep, almost mystical love for Tregarth House, the rich farm land, the sleek cattle, the bright-eyed Romney Marsh sheep, the new plantations of fir trees coming up to their first thinning, she would deprive him of all these, certain that by doing so she was hurting him even harder than he had hurt her . . .

How could he have been so crazy as to risk everything merely to lay a woman? But at least he'd come to his senses in time.

.    .    .    .    .

In the middle of September, when cold nights and sharp winds had coloured the woods and the grass had stopped growing, the phone rang in Tregarth House and Judith answered the call. It was for her husband. She said he was up at the cowshed and pressed the call switch for the extension line. 'Julian, there's a Mrs Smith on the line for you.'

42

He tensed as he stood in the small office beyond the parlour.

'Putting you through.'

There was a click. He heard Judith say: 'You're through.' There was another click as Judith replaced the receiver.

'Are you there, Julian?' asked Avis.

'What d'you want?'

'That makes for a charming welcome! I've been expecting to hear from you for weeks.'

'Why?'

'Oh! It's like that, is it? You got what you wanted and so there's an end to everything?'

He said nothing.

'You do realise, don't you, that I'm not some simple-minded milk-maid you can bounce in a hay-stack and then forget?'

'It'll be better for both of us if we do forget.'

She spoke mockingly: 'It'll be better for you if you realise we're seeing each other again, or else . . .'

'Or else what?'

'Or else Judith will learn quite a lot of new facts about her precious husband.'

'She won't believe a word,' he said with certainty.

'Not even when I show her the necklace that you were meant to buy for her but instead bought for me?'

Somehow, he'd forgotten all about that necklace. He suffered a feeling of empty, dry sickness, as if in a lift which had dropped too fast, too far.

'Kevin's going up to London next Tuesday to see his publisher. So we'll meet that night. Come here, to Honey Cottage. I know it'll be slumming for you, but at least I won't have to register as Mrs Smith.'

'Avis, please . . .'

'In the evening, any time after eight.' She rang off.

He replaced the receiver. He daren't go to the house. He daren't not go to the house. He stared out through the window at the large Dutch barn, filled with three thousand two hundred bales of top quality hay. No over-ambitious bitch was going to take that – and all it stood for – away from him.

# 8

Maude Bowring lived in one of the northern suburbs of Hemscross, in a small terrace house. Over the past years she had put on a great deal of weight and was now unmistakably fat. Her face suggested a contented, characterless nature.

She opened the front door to find that her caller was Powell. She said: 'Hullo, Bert, how are you?' as calmly as if she had last seen her brother weeks instead of years before. 'Come on in.'

He stepped into the hall and handed her a package. 'It's some chocolate for the kids.'

She spoke uncertainly. 'Teddy's married. I suppose you knew?'

'No, I didn't.'

'And Ruth's doing nursing up in London: getting on real well.'

He gestured with his hand. 'I hadn't realised how old they'd become. You'll have to eat the chocolates yourself.'

'There's no hardship in that! . . . You'll need a cup of tea.'

They went through to the kitchen because it didn't occur to her to have a mid-morning cup of tea anywhere else. He looked round and noted the broken tiles above the sink, the battered units which didn't match, and the refrigerator which had been badly scratched down almost the whole length of the door.

'We keep seeing photos in the local paper of you

and Judith,' she said proudly. 'Who'd ever of imagined that one of the family'd become famous?'

He tried to hide his impatience.

'Not so long ago there was a big picture of Judith looking ever so smart and I said to Mike, if you'd of told me forty years ago that my brother, Bert, would live in a huge house and own a big estate, I'd of told you you was bonkers.' She opened a cupboard and brought out an old, slightly rusty tea-caddy.

'How is Mike?'

'Beginning to feel the job's a bit much for him, but none of us are getting any younger. It's the arthritis. Had it for years and the doctors can't seem to do anything but tell him he's got to put up with it. Gets him down, sometimes.'

He couldn't remember anything about his brother-in-law except that he was forever sniffing.

She studied him. 'You don't look all that fit, Bert.'

'Julian,' he corrected her.

'I always forget you changed your name. There's been a Bert in the family ever since great-grandad.'

'Has there?'

'Mum told me that. She used to know everything about the family . . .' She chatted on. She made the tea and poured it into two chipped mugs, one of which she passed to him, and put a bottle of milk and a plastic container of sugar on the table. 'Have a biscuit? I've some of them garibaldies what you used to like so much.'

He refused, wondering how she could remember what he had liked or disliked all those long years ago.

'So how's the farm going?'

He took the trouble briefly to answer her question and was surprised to see the look of longing on her face. Clearly, her heart still lay in the countryside.

'Maude, I want to get in touch with Reginald,' he said finally. 'Where's he living now?'

'I . . . I don't know whether you heard? He was sent to . . . to prison.'

'Is he still in jail?' he asked harshly.

She imagined he was angry because of the shame of having a brother jailed. 'They let him out early under a scheme where he got a job and just reported back at night, but even that's finished with now.'

'What had he done?'

'He kind of got mixed up with a wild bunch. If he hadn't, he'd never of done such things: I know he wouldn't.'

'What sort of things?'

'Stealing wages and hitting the guards,' she said, her voice low. She was surprised to see his tight expression relax.

.     .     .     .     .

Reginald Powell was five feet eleven tall, broad shouldered, and still slim waisted: his face was chunky and coarse and an inch long scar ran down his right cheek to add a touch of harshness to what would otherwise have been sly features.

He stared at Powell with an astonishment which turned to open hatred. 'What's brought you slumming?'

'I want a word with you.'

'It's a pity the feeling ain't mutual.'

When Powell said nothing more, his brother finally stepped to one side, shrugging his shoulders scornfully. They went into the front room. This was small, over-furnished, and it smelled of stale cigarette smoke and beer. A woman was sprawled in one of the arm-

47

chairs: her hair was aggressively blonde, her face thick with make-up, and the expression in her tired brown eyes suggested that all her illusions about life had long since been shattered. She looked at Powell with little interest.

Reginald Powell went over to the fireplace, kicking an empty pack of cigarettes across the worn and soiled carpet as he did so. 'What's there to talk on?'

'I've come to make a proposition.'

He turned towards the woman. 'Take a walk, Flo.'

'But I've been . . .'

'Move.'

She stood and left, her expression resentful: she still sometimes knew a tiny flicker of pride.

They heard the front door slam shut and then through the dingy net curtain and fly-blown window they saw her cross the road and walk along the pavement.

'I need help,' said Powell quietly.

'You what? I've needed help enough times in the past, but I ain't come running to you for it.' Reginald Powell's scornful anger grew. 'I'd of got more help from the splits than you. Heard I've been in the nick recent?'

'Yes, but let's forget all that . . .'

'We don't forget nothing, not when you come crawling for help after keeping right clear of me for thirty years. Didn't want to know whether I was alive or dead because you're the rich Mr Powell and if I'd of asked you to come and see me in the nick you'd've told me to get lost. But now you're in trouble and maybe me being an ex-con could be useful so you're all for forgetting. What's the play? Something you're scared to touch with your own white hands? I'll tell you. Get bloody lost.'

'There's a thousand quid in it for you.'

Reginald Powell's expression didn't lose its hatred, but it additionally became calculating. 'What are you handing out a grand for?'

'For breaking into a house and taking enough stuff to make it look like an ordinary burglary. All I'll want out of it will be a necklace.'

'What's that worth?'

'Six hundred pounds.'

'Who's going to be there?'

'Just one woman.'

'Why no one else? Ain't she married?'

'Her husband will be in London for the night.'

'Where's the house?'

'In the country. It's surrounded by farm land and screened by trees. The nearest neighbour is half a mile up the road.

'Is the house wired?'

'For electricity? Yes, of course – '

'For alarms, you stupid bastard.'

'Almost certainly not,' said Powell stiffly.

'All right, the job's dead easy: so why don't you do it yourself?'

'The woman . . . She knows me.'

His brother laughed jeeringly.

'You break into the house just after eight in the evening – '

'Are you round the twist? Two in the morning.'

'Just after eight. That way it makes certain she's the only one there.'

Reginald Powell ran his right finger along the scar on his cheek. 'If I was to be interested, it would cost three grand.'

They bargained, dislike and contempt making them

even more pugnacious than they would otherwise have been, and it was over a quarter of an hour before they agreed on the sum of two thousand, one thousand in advance, one thousand to be paid on delivery of the necklace.

# 9

Reginald Powell had none of his brother's sharp intelligence, drive, or determination. If he had stayed on the land he would have become the kind of farm-hand who needed to be closely supervised but who, when supervised, was a good worker: since he had drifted to the towns, where he knew no roots, and had neither the skill nor application to train for and hold down a good job, and since he blamed the world for his shortcomings, it was hardly surprising that he had drifted into crime.

He was not a successful criminal: cunning made a poor substitute for intelligence and application. Only a stupid man would have chosen Jock Anderson as an only accomplice, simply because his services came cheaply.

Anderson had been born into a family of nine children. His father had spent more time in prison than out of it – at least five of his brothers and sisters had been fathered by other men – and his mother, a selfish, weak-willed woman had simply not bothered about their upbringing. The schools he was supposed to have attended were grateful that he mostly played truant and he had committed his first real theft before he was eight. By the time he was twenty, he had a reputation as a moronic expert in violence. 'Snout,' a man had once said, 'would kill a month-old kid in its pram if you could get through to him that that's what you wanted.'

Reginald Powell didn't bother to explain the job

in anything but ludicrously general terms. 'It's a bloody walk-over, like doing a blind man. Just this broad in the house.'

Anderson nodded.

'There's a couple of centuries in it for you – are you on?'

He nodded again. He never worked out the feasibility of a job he was offered, realising the futility of this, but instead always said 'Yes' if he liked the man who gave the orders and he was being offered a large enough sum to see him through the foreseeable future, which was generally about a fortnight.

'Then to-morrow you take this car and case the scene.'

'O.K.' Anderson had a large, round head: his cheekbones were prominent, imparting a Slavonic look to his thick, crude features. He watched a woman come along the pavement towards the car and he felt horny: he usually did.

Reginald Powell lit a cheroot. He wondered why his brother wanted that necklace so desperately and how much extra he'd be able to black out of the bastard before handing it over.

. . . . .

On Tuesday morning, Scott pulled on the coat and thought vaguely that his only suit was getting old and soon he really must buy himself a new one.

'Aren't you ready?' Avis shouted from the hall.

He looked at his watch. 'There's plenty of time.' He wondered why she was so on edge to-day. He shrugged his shoulders. He picked up his ancient briefcase in which he'd packed pyjamas, toothbrush and toothpaste, and a change of underclothes, and went downstairs.

She was fidgeting with something by the telephone. 'What train are you coming back on?'

'The four-eighteen to-morrow. Unless I ring to the contrary because Charles wants to discuss film rights.'

'You've had an offer?'

'Not yet, but I remain optimistic.'

'You're just like a child,' she said angrily, 'living in day dreams . . . For God's sake, come on.' She hurried out of the house.

He followed her after locking the inner front door and leaving the key hidden in the porch. Living in day dreams? They helped to make life more bearable.

He opened the garage doors, lifting the right-hand one because the hinges had sprung and otherwise it scraped badly on the ground: by the time he'd finished, he saw that she'd settled in the driving seat. He wondered if she'd decide to drive to assert herself – but he didn't particularly like driving and never bothered who was at the wheel. He sat in the front passenger seat and she started the engine and backed out of the garage much faster than was necessary. It was supposed to be men who found in cars all sorts of hidden releases but Avis, he was certain, found a car a handy means of working off frustrations.

She drove on to the road at speed, careless of the possibility of another car coming along, and they were doing seventy by the time they were abreast of the old orchard. When they stopped at the cross-roads which marked the village, a woman carrying a heavy shopping basket began to cross the road. Avis hooted.

'We've still over twenty minutes in which to get to the station,' he said.

She ignored him. The moment the woman was clear, she drew out, turning left, and accelerated fiercely.

53

He wondered again, but only vaguely, what was disturbing her.

She didn't speak until they were passing a small copse of chestnut, the growth still bushy because the trees had been cut for stakes only four years before.

'What are you going to do to-night?' she asked.

'I thought I might go to a film.'

'Suppose the flat isn't empty after all – what then?'

It was unlike her to bother about such problems. 'There's always the put-u-up which gives one the illusion of sleeping . . . But Ted was quite certain he was going up to Scotland for the week.'

'Why hasn't he ever got married?'

'I wouldn't know.' But he had a shrewd idea: Edward Garth knew too much about the marriages of his friends.

They reached the outskirts of Ferington, crossed the bridge over the river and almost immediately the much larger bridge over the railway lines, turned right into the station car-park.

He climbed out. 'I'll see you at five-twenty to-morrow.'

'You told me you were catching the five-eighteen.'

'Four-eighteen, then I avoid the rush hour.'

She drove off and his last view of her was in profile with her mouth, which could be so filled with laughter, set in sullen lines. He began to climb the two flights of stairs which led up to the booking complex that ran above the lines.

# 10

Avis, in the sitting-room, poured herself out a second whisky and thought about Tregarth House. It was a pile of a building, but if nothing could be done about the exterior, a great deal could be done about the interior. Judith had decorated and furnished it with her own brand of dowdiness, yet taste and a lot of money could make the rooms quite elegant. . .

.    .    .    .    .

It was now dark and the car's headlights turned the thorn hedges, set high up on steep earth banks, into the side vaulting of a tunnel.

They reached Colderton cross-roads. Light was streaming out from the pub on the opposite corner and several cars were badly parked along the road. Reginald Powell visualised a foaming pint of beer: at the beginning of a job his mouth and throat always dried – this wasn't a sign of fear, merely a physical reaction over which he had absolutely no control.

'Straight over and then turn left fifty yards on,' said Anderson.

They crossed and passed the pub, just catching the high notes of a rough sing-song, cleared the last of the parked cars, and turned left.

'It's a mile down this road, on the right. The entrance is immediately past the tree.' Anderson had drawn a sketch map and on this he'd placed the ash tree which marked the position where the road bent very slightly to the right, ten yards before the drive entrance.

Their headlights picked out the ash tree. Reginald Powell braked and turned into the drive. The woman might hear their arrival, but because the ordinary person expected the world to continue as it always had and therefore violent trouble only happened to someone else, it was probable that she would find no cause for alarm.

He turned and backed, to park the car facing the road. They left, shutting the doors quietly. They had been wearing gloves from the start and now they brought nylon hoods out of their pockets, but did not yet pull these over their heads because it was a moonless night and dark.

Anderson led the way. The drive, badly surfaced, suddenly narrowed into a path as it met the thorn hedge which encircled the garden. He opened the wooden gate, not quite succeeding in stilling the squeaks. As he stepped on to the brick path, he could just make out a door now facing him. He hesitated, but Reginald Powell prodded him on. The room beyond was in darkness whilst light was coming from the house from around the corner: since the path went round the house, it was easy to guess that the door used as the front door was on the south facing side.

They donned their hoods, now there was enough light. They walked quickly to pass through the light from the windows, uneasy at being outlined even though they knew that to the south the house faced only woods. They could see that the hall was empty.

Both outer and inner porch doors were unlocked. Once inside, they heard the sounds of a man's talking, but the tones of his speech, and then a short passage of music, convinced them they were listening either to the television or radio.

Reginald Powell took a cut-throat razor from his coat pocket and flicked it open: at close quarters, people were more terrified by cold steel than by a gun. He nodded at Anderson, who would initially remain in the hall, then lifted the latch of the wooden door, pulled the door open, and stepped inside.

The settee was set caterwise, between the doorway and the very large ingle-nook fireplace, and Avis was sitting in the right-hand corner of it, watching the television. She was startled by the sudden opening of the door, but because she was expecting Powell she was not immediately frightened. Then she turned and she saw a thickset man whose face was flattened and made monstrous by a nylon mask and she was utterly terrified. Her first reactions were ones over which she had no control. She'd been holding the jade seahorse necklace and as she tried to force herself back into the settee – in the child-like, intuitive belief that if only she could make herself smaller, she'd make herself safer – she jammed her right hand down between the seat cushion and the arm of the settee. She opened her mouth to scream.

He came forward and held the razor in front of her face. 'Keep quiet, lady, so as there won't be no trouble.'

She slumped, as if every bone in her body had suddenly given way, and moaned.

'There ain't no one can hear you if you do scream, but I've sensitive ears.'

Her mouth was open as if she had difficulty in breathing and there was a glazed look in her eyes.

He turned off the television, then whistled twice and there was an answering whistle from the hall to tell him that Anderson was starting a quick search of the house. 'Where's your jewellery?'

She might not have heard.

'Come on, lady, make it easy for both of us. Where is it?'

She whispered: 'In . . . in a case in the cupboard in my bedroom.'

There was the sound of an approaching vehicle and she looked with desperate hope at the drawn curtains, but it became obvious it was passing on the road.

Anderson came down the stairs and into the sitting-room. 'It's all clear . . .' He stopped as he saw Avis for the first time. He had never before seen a woman so sensually beautiful: for him, her terrified defence-lessness exaggerated her desirability and he knew sharp, demanding desire.

Reginald Powell, not astute enough to judge what might be going on in Anderson's mind, said: 'Keep her quiet. I'm going upstairs.'

As the door shut behind him Anderson came forward slowly: he was beginning to sweat and his breath was short, as if he had been running. He was within three feet of her when he stopped. He stared at her.

Reginald Powell returned to the room, an opened leather jewel case in his hand. 'Where d'you keep the rest?' he demanded roughly.

'They're . . . they're all I've got,' she answered.

The jewel case contained a small rope of pearls, a couple of diamond rings, a ruby eternity ring, a brooch, and a bracelet. 'See if she's wearing a necklace.'

Anderson grabbed the two collars of her blouse and pulled them apart, ripping off one of the buttons. It was obvious that under the silk slip she was not wearing a brassière.

'Lady,' said Reginald Powell, 'you're going to make life painful for yourself if you don't tell where the rest of the jewels are.'

She kept trying to speak, but the words would not form.

He brought the razor from his pocket with his left hand and flicked it open. 'Where's the other stuff?'

'In . . . in . . . in the chest-of-drawers . . . It's only costume . . .'

He put the jewel box down and hurried out of the room.

Anderson reached out. She tried to break free to her left, across the settee, but he grabbed hold of her. He pulled violently at the right strap of her slip and the blue embroidered nylon fell away to reveal her breast. He cupped the smooth flesh and his sweating fingers plucked at the nipple.

She screamed.

He hit her, knocking her sideways to the floor. He followed her down, conscious of nothing beyond the fire in his groin. She screamed again and he put one hand over her mouth and the other on her throat, to quieten her. She gave a convulsive jerk and collapsed.

Reginald Powell slammed open the door and rushed into the room, razor at the ready. He stared at Avis, sprawled on the floor, and at Anderson, crouched over her, and he cursed wildly.

Anderson slowly came to his feet.

She hadn't moved. Reginald Powell pushed past Anderson, knelt, and began to shake her. Her head rolled from side to side.

'She must've fainted,' muttered Anderson thickly.

She was dead.

# 11

'I was only trying to keep her quiet,' said Anderson. 'So what do we do now, Reg?'

Reginald Powell gripped the handle of the razor so tightly that his knuckles whitened. Having killed her because his concrete-thick brain hadn't room for more than one idea at a time . . . They didn't top people now, but death in furtherance of rape was murder and certain of a life sentence with probably a minimum of twenty years to serve. Ten years inside made a bloke stir-crazy . . .

'I didn't know she was weak, did I?' said Anderson, now sounding aggrieved.

Reginald Powell relaxed his grip, folded the razor and dropped it into his pocket. A murder hunt would start up the moment her body was discovered . . . The car had been nicked, so there could be no lead there: no one had seen them arrive, no one would see them leave . . . Bert would know who'd murdered her, but he couldn't tell the splits without exposing himself. Or could he? Suppose he were really smart and went to the splits and strung 'em a tale about seeing his brother around the district recently . . . There wasn't a split alive who wouldn't believe a rich man rather than a poor man, especially when the poor man was an ex-con . . . How to make certain his brother didn't get a chance to finger them? Suppose nothing was left behind – like that button on the carpet – and then they faked an accident . . .

Because he was cunning but not intelligent, he did

not try to work out what the consequences of his idea might be.

.  .  .  .  .

They drove from Colderton to Stern Head, using minor roads which Reginald Powell remembered from his youth, in the two cars – the stolen Ford and Avis's Jaguar.

A spur of the Downs reached the sea to the west of Leatham, ending in four cliffs, the highest of which was three hundred and thirteen feet. Once isolated, these cliffs had become in the summer a favourite picnic site for trippers. Where once there had been weed grass, gorse, and the occasional tree, there were now painted wooden railings, a car park, litter bins, public lavatories, and concessional stalls. But by the middle of September, the stalls were shut and padlocked and except on a really sunny day not many people went there.

The Jaguar and the Ford drove into the car park, which was empty. The ground rose to a crown and then descended gently: they parked on the crown and climbed out of the cars. They could just make out the heavy, painted wooden fencing and the jagged cliff edge. Out to sea, green and white side and masthead lights marked ships steaming down Channel, much closer inshore a wreck buoy flashed green.

There was a strong wind, gusting heavily, and Reginald Powell had almost to shout to make himself heard. 'Get the jack and spring the driving door.'

It was difficult to work out how to anchor the base of the jack, but eventually, and after using a shielded light, they solved the problem. They forced the door of the Jaguar until it could no longer be closed.

61

Reginald Powell dropped a three parts empty bottle of whisky on to the back seat and Avis's handbag on to the front passenger seat.

Anderson climbed in behind the wheel. He switched on, engaged drive, released the handbrake, and accelerated. The Jaguar went down the shallow slope and slammed into the wooden railings to splinter its way through, picking up speed far more quickly than he had reckoned. He pushed open the driving door, finding some difficulty in overcoming the wind resistance, and threw himself out. Momentum rolled him over and forward. Desperately, he dug down with his feet into the soft soil. There was one last roll, which he thought was going to take him over, and then he came to a stop, his right hand dangling in space.

.    .    .    .    .

Dinner at Tregarth House was usually a formal occasion. On the long refectory table were set three-forked Georgian candelabra, with candles lit, a heavy silver gilt epergne, queen's pattern cutlery, Waterford crystal, and damask napery. On the nights when Olive Bins waited at table there was an air of pretentiousness about the scene: when they waited on themselves, a suggestion of farce was added. But it ceased to be ridiculous if one remembered that eight-year-old child who had sworn to himself that one day he would lead the life of the rich and then had had the courage and the staying power to make it come true.

This Tuesday they were on their own and Judith had just brought in the cold salmon, mayonnaise, and boiled potatoes, when the phone rang. 'Answer it, will you, Julian? I've still the peas to dish,' she said, before she realised he was already passing through the doorway.

He crossed the drawing-room and went into the study, careful to close the door. He had no premonition of disaster, but was on edge because he still couldn't decide how long to leave it before he rang Avis to apologise for not being able to get along that evening.

He lifted the receiver. It was not until the question, 'Are you on your own?' was repeated that he realised it was his brother's voice.

'How did it go?' he demanded.

'It blew up. We've made it look like an accident. Keep your mouth tight shut and it'll stay an accident, open it and you'll be in more trouble than you've ever thought of because I'm not sinking without taking you with me. Got it?'

'What have you made look like an accident?'

'Her being dead, you soft bastard. So just forget everything and keep right away from me. Have you been in the house all evening?'

'Yes,' he croaked.

'So who's been there with you?'

'Judith . . . all the time . . . and the farm manager was here half an hour ago . . .'

'Keep on remembering, if the splits get a hand on my collar, I'll see they get two hands on yours.' The line went dead.

He replaced the receiver, shocked and physically weak, and sat on the padded arm of the nearest chair.

'Julian,' he heard Judith call, 'Hurry it up, the meal's all ready.'

They'd made it look like an accident. If her death had not, in fact, been an accident, had it then been murder?

Judith came into the library. 'Didn't you hear . . . My God!' she blurted out as she saw his face. 'Are you ill?' She hurried to him and drew his head against her side in an instinctive gesture of protection. 'Shall I call the doctor?'

He had to give an explanation that would allay any possible suspicions. 'It . . . it was some man telling me that he was going to kill me because I'm a capitalist.'

Her expression changed as she could not avoid a feeling of critical surprise that he should so allow a crank telephone call to upset him. 'Ridiculous.' She tried to speak more sympathetically. 'Get on to the police and tell them what's happened.'

'I don't . . . I don't think that's a good idea.'

'Of course you've got to phone them.' She lifted the receiver.

'They won't bother about a crank call . . .'

She dialled 999. The police asked her to get in touch with the local divisional station and gave her the number. She spoke to the duty sergeant, then passed the phone across. 'They want a word with you. Would you like a whisky?'

He nodded.

'Hullo, Mr Powell,' said the sergeant, 'I understand you've had an unpleasant phone call. Will you tell me exactly what was said?'

'It's . . . it's all a bit jumbled for me now.'

'That's not at all surprising. When something like this happens, it shocks anyone up. But just do the best you can.'

'He said I was a capitalist so he's going to kill me.'

'He gave no other explanation?'

'No.'

'I suppose you didn't recognise the voice?'

'No.'

'There was just this one threat?'

'Yes.'

'If you employ people in your house or your work, have you recently had occasion to sack anyone?'

'I've a farm, but everyone who works on it has been with me for years.'

'I see. Now, were there any special characteristics about the call – did it come straight through or were there the pips which show it's coming from a call-box?'

'There were pips.'

'That's to be expected since most calls like this come through a call-box . . . Well, we'll make a note of what's happened and report the matter to the telephone people, but frankly at this stage there's not very much else we can do. But if you should receive another call like this one, will you tell us about it straight away? If someone's got it in for you and keeps making calls, then between the post office and ourselves we might be able to nab him. Sorry you've had the bother, but don't get concerned about it. It'll only be some nutter.' There was a quick chuckle. 'At least you were spared someone trying out his four letter vocabulary.'

Judith returned with a drink as he replaced the receiver. 'Here you are. It'll make you feel better.'

A whole bottle couldn't do that, he thought despairingly.

# 12

After the detective had left Honey Cottage on the Thursday morning, Scott stared through the rain-streaked window of the sitting-room and watched him hurrying through the wet to his car. Fiona was mentally ill, he thought bitterly.

He walked into the hall and round the foot of the stairs to the corner cupboard on which the phone stood. If Avis were not with Fiona as he'd assumed – and therefore had not been worried by her absence – where was she? Could she have gone to stay with the Ambridges or the Thomases?

Claire Ambridge was polite enough to hide her astonishment: Mary Thomas was boisterously vulgar and asked him what he hadn't been doing to Avis to make her run away.

He returned upstairs and sat at the typewriter, but his mind refused to settle back to work. Fiona must realise that if Avis found something better to do she would never put off the doing of it just because of a prior appointment – and probably Fiona even understood that Avis would let her down for the malicious pleasure of knowing the disappointment this would cause. So something more must have been running through her sick mind. She'd mentioned Jane to the police. Had Avis been voicing her ridiculous suspicions, garnered from God knows where, and had Fiona accepted them seriously, so that she believed he might have cause to murder Avis . . . ?

.     .     .     .     .

Bratby, six years retired, walked his dog every morning and afternoon, rain or shine. Dressed in wellingtons, leggings, oilskins, and a battered sou'-wester, he rounded a rock spur and through the sheeting rain he saw something out to sea, about thirty yards from the water's edge, which was wedged against a single tongue of rock. He squinted slightly as he identified a badly crushed car.

'Come on, Bruce,' he said to the dog, 'we'd better go and tell the police.' He enjoyed anything which broke up the humdrum of retired life.

.    .    .    .    .

At low neap tide the sand stretched for an unbroken two miles and the break-down truck, with a P.C. in the passenger seat, was able to drive round to the point where the shattered car lay, still against the single pinnacle of rock, in less than two feet of water.

The P.C., who was wearing thigh-length sea-boots, checked the collar of his mackintosh and then stepped out on to the sand. The third law of police investigations, he thought sourly, stated that if rain would make a job more disagreeable, it rained.

The winch was in neutral. He reached up and took hold of the heavy steel hook and, unwinding the wire, carried it into the sea. The small waves slapped against his legs, sending quick spurts of spray springing upwards. He reached the wrecked car, secured the hook, stepped clear, and waved. There was the tooth-twingeing sound of metal scraping against rock as the car was pulled clear, then amidst a flurry of water, it was winched ashore.

The P.C. looked inside the shattered car and found, thankfully, that there was no even more shattered

67

body inside. The driver climbed down from the truck. 'So where d'you think it came from?'

'Could be Stern Head. There was a report that the rails in the car-park had been smashed.'

'Went over there, eh? So all we've got to do now is get it to your place?' The driver whistled a few bars from one of the latest pop tunes. 'We'll have to get one end up on the trolley, then trail it. Bloody awful job.'

Some blokes could never stop moaning, thought the P.C., as a cold trickle of rain began to slide down his back.

. . . . .

Ferington central police station, built five years before, was ten storeys high, with its main entrance one storey up and approached by a wide sweeping ramp.

Kelly's office was on the third floor. It was a square room with light green walls, white ceiling, and a very large picture window, double glazed, which to his perpetual annoyance couldn't be opened because the building was fully air-conditioned: there were times, especially when the paperwork became mountainous, when he longed to hurl a chair through the window so that he could breathe fresh air.

The telephone rang. 'D.S.'

'Sarge, there's a report from B div. They've hauled a car out of the sea which probably went over the edge at Stern Head. No body inside, but the driving door has sprung. The registration number identifies the owner as Mrs Avis Scott who lives at Honey Cottage, Colderton.'

'I suppose they're putting the car through Vehicle Testing?'

'I couldn't answer that one.'

He replaced the receiver, leaned back in his chair, and thought about Scott. A man who covered up his feelings under an air of detached irony, strongly committed to personal privacy. It seemed obvious that his marriage was not a happy one. People! But for them, the world could have been a happy place. Because his work brought him constantly in contact with crime and misery, he sometimes felt as if the overriding obsession of the human race was to destroy the slightest pleasure in living. Yet he was totally content with life, having a home, a wife, and a family. Perhaps that merely pointed to a lack of ambition: but having so often seen the tragic consequences of ambition, he was quite content to lack it.

.      .      .      .      .

At four-thirty, Scott finally gave up trying to write any more that day and he went downstairs to make some coffee. While in the kitchen he heard a car turn into the drive and he hurried through to the dining-room to look through the north facing window. He saw Kelly climb out of a car, adjust the collar of his mackintosh, and walk towards the gate.

When he opened the outside porch door, Kelly said quietly: 'I'm sorry to interrupt you again, but I've some serious news. I'm afraid your wife's car has been pulled out of the sea: there was no one inside it. We think it went over the edge at Stern Head.'

Shocked, Scott said nothing.

'May I come in?' Kelly hung his dripping mackintosh on one of the hooks in the porch, then stepped into the hall. 'I'm going to have to ask you a whole lot more questions.'

Wordlessly, Scott opened the sitting-room door. At that moment the kettle began to whistle and he went through to the kitchen to switch it off. On his return, he found Kelly was standing in the centre of the room.

'Mr Scott, was your wife at all depressed when you last saw her?'

'No,' he answered thickly.

'Had you had a row?'

'No.'

'Then how would you describe relations between you and your wife on Tuesday morning?'

'How I described them this morning. . . .' His voice became clipped. 'You said no one was in the car. Do you . . . believe she was in it when it crashed?'

'I'm very much afraid that for the moment one has to assume that.'

There was a short silence, broken by Kelly. 'Your wife drove you to the station on Tuesday morning – was she her normal self?'

'Yes.'

'You're quite certain?'

'She may have been slightly on edge, that's all.'

'What was the reason for that?'

'I've no idea.'

'And when you caught the train on Tuesday you expected her to meet you at the station on Wednesday afternoon?'

'Yes.'

'When you returned here, how did you find things – had the post been read, was the milk taken in?'

'Wednesday's post was in the porch, where the post-man leaves it: the day's milk was out in the small container by the garage.'

'Does your wife have her own bank or savings accounts?'

'She banks at the high street branch of the National Westminster.'

'Does she have a private income?'

'Her father left her some money.'

'Can you tell me whether this was a large amount?'

'It was about thirty thousand pounds.'

'I imagine that after I left you in the morning, you rang a number of friends to find out if your wife was staying with them?'

'Yes.'

'But without result?'

'Yes.'

'Has Mrs Ballentyne had any word from her?'

'Why bring her name into it?'

'I wondered if you'd considered the possibility that your wife might have made contact with her?'

'I haven't.'

'Where does Mrs Ballentyne live?'

'In Ferington.'

'D'you mind giving me her address?'

'Flat six b, Norwood House. But she doesn't know anything about Avis.'

'In a case like this we have to check all possible leads. Please believe me, Mr Scott, I dislike having to ask these questions just as much as you dislike having them asked.'

The detective left almost immediately afterwards. Scott stayed in the sitting-room. Even though he'd ceased to love Avis, it still hurt to think of her as dead.

# 13

There were three back doors to Tregarth House: for the tradesmen, for the indoor servants, and for the gardeners and grooms. Powell usually used the indoor servants' entrance, not because of the ironic pleasure this could give him but because it was easy to leave his boots and raincoat in the passage and go straight through to the kitchen.

Judith was stirring the contents of a saucepan which was on the oil-fired Aga. 'What a terrible day! If this is autumn, I hate to think what winter's going to be like. Did you manage to finish the field?'

'Yes.'

She turned. 'You're surely not still upset about that phone call?'

'Of course not,' he answered irritably. 'I was worrying about the land and how to get everything done with all this wet.'

She accepted the explanation. 'By the way, Julian, Mrs French says that the rumour's going round the village that something's happened to Avis.'

'What?' he said loudly.

'You startled me! . . . They say that Avis has been in some sort of very serious car accident. I do hope it isn't true, but I think you ought to ring Kevin.'

'Why?'

'That's a ridiculous question. To find out if anything has happened to her, of course, and if it has to see how we can help.'

'It'll only be one of those absurd rumours which are always going around.'

She spoke sadly. 'You don't like helping other people, do you?'

. . . . .

Kelly yawned and wondered when was the last time he had managed to be up-to-date with the work? In the old days there had been poverty and hardship and so, except to the very narrow minded, there had been an excuse for much of the crime. But now, when poverty had been virtually abolished, the crime figures seemed forever to increase. A rising standard of living had not brought the contented happiness it should have done . . .

The detective inspector came into the room. Craven – an unsuitable name for a man of physical and moral courage – was tall and thin, with a hard, lean face. He was a firm disciplinarian who, like Kelly, had little time for the permissive age, but otherwise his standards were different ones. He sat on the edge of the battered desk. 'How's the hit-and-run job looking?'

'We've been in contact with every local garage, but none of them report a green Ford Capri with damaged left front: no headlamp units have recently been sold locally.'

'It was a local car.'

Kelly shrugged his shoulders. The evidence, such as it was, was ambiguous on that point.

'Keep plugging away.'

They both knew little more time could be given to the case.

'Anything more on the car which went over Stern Head?'

73

'I'm waiting on Vehicle Testing.'

'Chivvy 'em up on the phone.'

Kelly pushed the telephone across the desk. 'Rank carries clout. The number's three six one nine four two, sir.'

The D.I. began to dial. He liked and respected the detective sergeant, even though he had written in Kelly's confidential report the damning letters N.S.F.P. Not suitable for further promotion. He spoke to a P.C. who tried to plead pressure of work, but he refused to be sidetracked. He listened to what a second man had to say, thanked the other, and rang off. 'The usual excuses: they've a hundred and one vehicles in and half the staff off sick with the plague. But they have managed a superficial examination and there's one point of interest. The driving door shows marks which suggest something had been used to spring it.'

Kelly began to tap on the desk with his fingers, a habit of his which so annoyed his wife. 'Forced the door, sent the car on its way, kept the body back for hiding elsewhere. That way there's no body to cry murder, but there is a very good reason for its absence.'

'What's the husband like?'

'His own worst enemy: smart but unhappy and tries to conceal the fact under a flip manner. He's a writer. My wife got one of his books out of the library yesterday and began to read it: she says it isn't the kind of book you want when you're tired and need to relax.'

'Was he having trouble with the wife?'

'Some trouble, yes, but I've no idea how much. Incidentally, she was left a bit of money by her father.'

'What d'you call a bit of money?'

'Thirty thousand quid.'

74

'You're becoming blasé. If I were left thirty thousand, I'd call myself rich.'

'Another thing, there's a second woman around.'

'Have you seen her?'

'I was keeping her until the report from Vehicle Testing.'

Craven slid off the desk. 'It's beginning to sound like a recipe for murder.'

.    .    .    .    .

Scott parked the car he had had to rent in the council car-park. He bought a pack of cigarettes from a vending machine, then carried on to Norwood House. It was a tower block, but for once the architect had managed to add a sense of grace: additionally, the garden was tended by a man who paid more heed to results than to his hours and so it was usually filled with colour.

He stepped into the recessed entrance and pressed the button for 6b. Jane's voice, sounding hollow through the speaker, asked him to identify himself.

'Kevin!' Her surprise was obvious. There was a quick buzz and the front door opened.

The lift took him to the sixth floor. She had changed into sweater and a pair of slacks and her hair looked as if she had recently been out in the wind. 'I didn't expect to see you here,' she said, her words mildly reproving.

He stepped into the tiny hall. 'Something's cropped up which I decided I had to talk over with you.'

She briefly studied his face, then turned and led the way into the sitting-cum-dining-room. 'Will you have a drink? The cellar's very limited, but it can run to sherry or gin with tonic or bitters.'

'Sherry would be fine.'

She went over to a small sideboard, poured out the drinks, and handed him a glass. 'You won't mind if I'm very frank, will you?' she said, as she sat on a pouf near one of the radiators. 'I'm always pleased to see you, but I'd rather that if you come here to the flat, you come with Avis. I'm afraid I'm hopelessly old fashioned: but I've probably told you that before.'

'I wouldn't be here if there weren't something you need to know about.'

'Fair enough. And as you're here, for heaven's sake grab a seat and stop standing around in a state of frigidity. . . .' She chuckled. 'That wasn't really what I meant to say. Steve always claimed that if it were possible for me to say the wrong thing at the wrong time, I would.'

He sat on one of the arm-chairs. 'Avis has disappeared.'

'You mean, she's left you?'

He shook his head. 'She's literally disappeared. And her car went over the cliff at Stern Head and has been recovered from the sea.'

'Oh, my God!' she exclaimed.

'The last time I saw her was when she dropped me at the station on Tuesday and I went up to London for the night. When I returned on Wednesday she should have met me, but didn't. She didn't turn up Wednesday night.

'One of her friends, Fiona Holloway, kept trying to get in touch with her and when she couldn't she got on to the police.' His voice sharpened. 'Fiona's a pretty sick character and she said some ridiculous things. One of them was that I was having an affair with you.'

Her anger was immediate. 'How does she dare say such a filthy lie? And who mentioned my name to her? Did you?'

'Of course not.'

'Then it was Avis?'

'I can't think it could have been anyone else.'

'Then why should Avis believe we're having an affair?'

'God knows! But for some reason, before she disappeared she began to get jealous.'

'Then she's just as sick as her friend . . . I'm sorry, I shouldn't have said that.' She stood up and went across to the picture window and stared out at the distant countryside. 'But it makes me furious when people are small and bitchy minded.'

'The police are trying to find out what's happened to Avis and a detective questioned me about you. He's probably going to come here to see you.'

'Isn't life wonderful!' She returned to the pouf and sat, very upright. 'So I'll tell him the truth and that'll knock that story back into the mud where it belongs.' She picked up her glass and drank, then said: 'I'm terribly sorry, Kevin, but I've been selfish enough to forget for the moment what's really happened. Maybe Avis's car was stolen and then sent over the cliff by the yobbos who pinched it. That sort of thing seems to be happening all the time these days.'

'If so, she'd have reported the car stolen.'

'Then she . . .' She shook her head. 'No, it's unkind to try to paint a better picture than the facts do. I learned that when Steve died. So all I'll say is, I hope it's not as serious as it looks. Or if it is . . .' She paused, then said in a rush: 'That it's not going to hurt as much as it might have done.'

77

'Thanks.'

'For implying something that is none of my business? Life can get very off-balance, can't it?' She abruptly changed the conversation.

# 14

Once a month, the detective chief superintendent at county H.Q. held a conference which had to be attended by all the detectives of the rank of detective inspector and above. A forum of ideas and suggestions, he called it. The forum tended to be restricted to his ideas and his suggestions.

At the end of the conference, Craven left the main building and made his way round to a second and much smaller one, attached by a covered way, which housed the vehicle section. On the ground floor was a large inspection area, with hoist and pit, lit by a battery of strip lights. A van, parked over the pit, was being examined by a couple of men in overalls. He edged his way past them and went into a small, cluttered office in which a uniform sergeant was typing.

'Have you anything more yet on the Jaguar that went over Stern Head?' Craven asked.

The sergeant searched through a pile of reports and found the one he wanted: he passed it across.

Craven read. The car had been crushed after falling from a great height on to rocks . . . Small pieces of wood, some painted white, had been wedged into the bonnet grille . . . A three parts empty bottle of whisky had survived the fall . . . A thread of material had been caught on the trailing edge of the driving door . . . Marks on the pillar and driving door suggested pressure had been applied, perhaps to spring the door . . .

A uniform inspector hurried into the office. 'Hullo, Tom, how's life?' Not waiting for an answer, he said to the sergeant: 'Where's all the guff on the caravan?'

'Forwarded to A division, sir.'

'I've just had 'em moaning like hell because they haven't got it.'

The telephone rang and the sergeant answered the call.

The inspector sighed as he brushed the back of his hand across his forehead. 'If I'm not growing a crop of ulcers, I'm a bloody medical miracle.' He went round behind the second desk and slumped down in the chair.

Craven tapped the sheet of paper in his hand. 'This Jaguar which went over Stern Head – what's it add up to?'

The inspector said heavily: 'It's all written down there. The door was sprung, probably with a jack, before the crash. The automatic gear shift was set at drive, but the lights weren't switched on. . . . Any idea of the time of day when the car went over?'

'Not before dark Tuesday night and not after eight-fifteen, Wednesday morning.'

'If it was dark, those lights could be significant.'

Craven spoke slowly. 'You'd have to be either crazy or tight, wouldn't you, to move a car up there without lights on? Has Dabs been over the wreck?'

'Yes, but his report's not through yet. I had a quick word with him, though, and he says there are no prints on the steering wheel or the bottle though there were smudges on both, perhaps from gloves.'

Mrs Scott presumably wore gloves from time to time, thought Craven, but normally the bottle would not have been handled in gloved hands unless, perhaps, she had picked it up on her way to the car. But

80

in those circumstances one would expect to find the finger-prints of past handlings.

'One last thing,' said the inspector. 'That short length of thread, caught in the edge of the car door, is probably from a tweedy coat containing a reddish brown colour.'

'All right if I take it back with me?'

'Just so long as you sign for it.' He spoke to the sergeant. 'Get the thread for Mr Craven, but don't let him out of your sight until he's signed a U four.'

.    .    .    .    .

Scott pushed the chair free of the table, stood up, and crossed to the window. If only the uncertainty would end.

The phone rang and he went downstairs.

'Is she there?'

He immediately recognised the croaking voice of Fiona Holloway. 'I'm afraid she hasn't come back and her car's been found in the sea after going over Stern Head.'

'You've murdered her,' she shouted.

'Don't be so bloody ridiculous. And why . . .'

'You won't get away with it. D'you understand that?' She cut the connexion.

He replaced the receiver, knowing a dull, sick sense of despair as he did so. Why was hatred often so much stronger and more enduring an emotion than love? Hatred seldom changed, love often did. Fiona had hated him from the day she'd first met him: he had initially loved Avis, yet soon that love had turned into a cynical resignation.

.    .    .    .    .

81

Kelly stood in the car park of Stern Head and watched the council workmen nail into position the last crosspiece of timber to complete the repairs to the rails. They collected up their tools and bundled together a number of pieces of wood, some of them nearly four feet long. That wood would never be returned to stores, Kelly knew: petty dishonesty had become a way of life. Yet petty dishonesty so often paved the way to serious dishonesty . . . What the hell! He'd soon be retiring on a pension and then he could grow championship roses and let the world go to hell in whichever way it wanted.

The workmen crossed to their van, climbed in, and drove off. Kelly walked down to the railings and then, with all the dread of a lifelong altophobe, he ducked under the lowest rail. As he studied the ground between the rails and the edge of the cliff a gust of wind, not particularly strong, forced him to readjust his balance. By mistake he looked beyond the cliff edge to the sea, a million miles below. He suffered an attack of giddiness which left him breathless. Why in the goddamn hell, he wondered despairingly, hadn't he sent one of the D.C.s along instead of being so pig-headedly determined to check for himself?

He hunkered down on his heels and examined the ground. It was damp and the car tracks were readily identifiable: they ran straight to the edge of the cliff – he assumed they reached the edge: he didn't dare look all the way – with no indication that the brakes had been slammed on in a desperate attempt to avoid going over. Of course, without the lights on the driver might not have known how close she was to disaster until the car had broken through the railings and then the whisky might have dulled her reactions sufficiently . . . But if she had been capable of driving at all, wouldn't she have instinctively switched on the lights . . . ?

Near the edge of the cliff – so near that he began to shake – there were other marks to the side of the tyre marks. The grass was crushed and there was a large, shallow depression and a smaller, deeper one. The kind of marks a man would make if he threw himself out of a car just before it went over the edge and he had to jam his toes into the ground to prevent the momentum taking him over as well?

He returned to the railings and the car park. He lit a cigarette, hoping it would help to calm his churning stomach. When he'd smoked it, he crossed to his car, switched on the transmitter, and spoke to the operations room at H.Q. to ask them to pass the message on to send out someone to take photos and make casts of the marks.

·       ·       ·       ·       ·

At ten-fifteen on Saturday morning, Kelly went to Norwood House. He immediately liked Jane Ballentyne. She was his kind of woman. Nothing showy, perhaps a trifle too much weight by modern standards, but with a warm, caring nature. 'I'm sorry to bother you, Mrs Ballentyne, but I've come along – '

'To question me regarding my friendship with Mr Scott?'

He nodded. She stepped aside and he entered her flat and followed her into the sitting-room. She stood with her back to the picture window. 'Have you found Mrs Scott?' she asked.

'Not yet. I'm afraid it may take rather a long time. If she was in her car, then the tides around Stern Head are very strong.'

'If it was an accident, why are you bothering to come here?' she asked almost curtly.

'We have to check up.'

'You don't believe it was an accident, do you?'

'I'm afraid I can't answer that because I simply don't know. Let me put things another way. Right now, there has to be the possibility that it wasn't an accident, simply because we know so little. So we're checking up and if we discover that it quite definitely was an accident, we can then scotch any rumours.'

She crossed to a chair and sat. 'I've never met Fiona Holloway, but even if she probably needs pitying rather than cursing, I'm sure she's dangerous.'

'Obviously Mr Scott has been here. He probably explained that Miss Holloway has alleged that Mr Scott and you have for some time been having an affair. Now as I see it, the only person from whom she could have gained such an idea was Mrs Scott . . .' He let his voice die away so that the unfinished sentence became a question.

'Avis has never had the slightest reason for believing that Kevin and I are anything more than casual friends,' she said angrily.

'You are quite certain of that?'

'Dammit, I . . .' She sighed. 'I suppose I'm incredibly naive for this day and age, but I can't understand why a man and a woman can't see each other occasionally, always in full public view, without the rest of the world assuming the worst.'

'Are you saying, then, that Mr Scott has never been in this flat?'

She nervously clasped her hands together around her knees. 'Kevin's been up here once so our meetings haven't all been in full public view. But it didn't extend beyond one glass of sherry and it happened this Thursday, two days after Avis disappeared – so it had no influence on the way she thought. And when we do see each other we discuss books and the most maiden of aunts could listen in and not blush once.'

'You've made things very clear, Mrs Ballentyne.' He smiled. 'Thanks for being so helpful.'

She looked up at him. 'I've told you the absolute truth.'

Emotionally, he believed her: but as a policeman, he wondered.

.   .   .   .   .

The front office of divisional H.Q. was one and a half floors high and separated into two by the long counter. In front of this counter were some uncomfortable chairs, a couple of tables on which were a selection of police pamphlets, and on the walls a series of posters recruiting, admonishing, advising.

Jenkins entered from outside and went up to the counter. He had a thin, pointed, furry face and his pale blue eyes were seldom still.

The duty sergeant studied him. 'I thought it was too much to hope for when they told me you'd gone to live in the West country.'

'Couldn't stand the people there, Sarge.'

'Kept catching you at it, did they?'

He chuckled, showing stained teeth.

'All right, then, let's hear what brings you in. And keep both your hands where I can see 'em.'

'I got to talking to Jimmy and he said . . .'

'Let's get things sorted out. Who's Jimmy?'

'Jimmy Williams, my local copper. And he said to come and talk to you.'

'That's earned him extra duty for a start.'

'There's been a rumour going around about Mrs Scott, the wife of the bloke what writes. Her car went over the edge, didn't it?'

'So?'

'Some people is saying there's something funny about her death.'

'Some people'll say anything.'

'I saw her car that night.'

'What time?'

'Just before nine: could've been five to.'

'How do you know it was her car?'

'I knows all the cars what are local.'

'Where were you?'

Jenkins tapped the side of his nose with his fore-finger and winked.

'Cut out the hamming.'

'Polgate Wood.'

'And pheasants not even in season yet,' said the sergeant disgustedly.

'She weren't driving.'

'Who was?'

'It were a man.'

'Could you see anything of him?'

'Only the back of his 'ead.'

'Was she in the car with him?'

'Couldn't see no one else.'

'Can you tell us anything more than that?'

'Can't. But thought you'd want to know, like.'

# 15

On Sunday Scott was in the kitchen, eating a late breakfast standing up, when Kelly arrived.

'Have you heard at all from Mrs Scott?' Kelly asked.

'Not a word.'

'I'm sorry. I'd hoped you would have done.'

Scott found it strange that the detective's manner remained so friendly when he suspected Avis had been murdered. But then perhaps all police work was a form of hypocrisy? 'Could you manage a coffee?'

'It would go down a treat.'

In the kitchen, Scott filled a fresh mug with coffee, then poured what remained in the espresso machine into his own. He passed the first mug across. 'Help yourself to milk and sugar and we'll go into the sitting-room.'

'Don't let me interrupt your breakfast.'

'I finished eating as you arrived.'

They went into the sitting-room and Scott switched on the fan heater. Kelly said: 'Cheers,' and drank. He lowered the mug. 'Last Tuesday you went up to London and spent the night there, didn't you?'

'Yes.'

'Where did you stay?'

'In a friend's flat.'

'Was he there?'

'No.'

'Then you were on your own?'

'That's right.'

'Did you go out in the evening?'

'I intended originally to go to a film, but in the event I couldn't be bothered.'

'Is there anyone who could vouch for you being in London that evening?'

'I saw no one I knew.'

'We've had a report through to the effect that your wife's car was on the road at around nine, being driven by a man. Can you suggest who that man might have been?'

'I'd say your report is a load of cod's. Avis wouldn't have let anyone else drive her car: half the time, she didn't even like my handling it.'

They both heard another car drive off the road and Scott crossed to the window. He didn't recognise the blue Ford Fiesta which had parked by the side of the detective's car.

'If you've a visitor, I'll get from under your feet.' Kelly finished his coffee in three quick swallows. 'By the way, if you do remember meeting anyone in London, say between seven-thirty and ten, let me know, will you?'

A woman climbed out of the car and when she stood upright Scott realised she was Jane.

Kelly went into the hall. He opened the inner porch door as Jane reached the outer one. His expression didn't alter as he moved to one side to let Scott get past him.

Scott said: 'Hullo, Jane: what an unexpected pleasure!'

She came through the porch: 'I was driving . . .' She stopped when she saw Kelly.

'Hullo again, Mrs Ballentyne,' said Kelly. 'Thanks for the coffee, Mr Scott.' He left.

As he went past the kitchen window, she said:

'You don't believe he'll think . . .' She became silent.

'He'll think the worst because that's what his job is all about,' replied Scott roughly.

'But when I set out for a spin I'd really no intention of coming here. It's just that I found myself at Colderton cross-roads and so decided to drop in for a moment.'

'Until Avis disappeared, I'd never realised how often the truth can become a lie.' He shrugged his shoulders. 'He'll think what he wants and there's nothing we can do about it, so come on into the sitting-room. Mind your head on the doorway: either they were all midgets when this place was built or else everyone perpetually went around with bowed shoulders.'

'I didn't know you lived in a lovely old cottage like this.'

'You've not been here before? Avis hated the place, but I've always loved it.'

She sat. 'I suppose he hasn't heard anything more about Avis?'

'No. He came and saw you, I take it?'

'Yesterday.'

She spoke evenly. 'He made one point, Kevin. Fiona surely could only have got the ridiculous idea from Avis. So why did she have it? It's not as if we've ever done anything that could remotely hint at an affair. Avis had absolutely no cause to think that about us, so why did she?'

'God knows, I don't.'

'But there has to be a reason.'

'Then I haven't a clue what it is.'

'If the detective thinks . . .' She came to a stop.

'If he thinks Avis did have reason for her belief,

if he's certain she's dead and it wasn't an accident, then he's convinced I had a very good motive for killing her.'

'It's like a nightmare . . . But surely the police know enough about people to be certain you wouldn't ever kill anyone?'

'I read a book recently, written by a retired policeman, which said that every single person can be attracted to crime in exceptional circumstances. So according to that, if I'm passionately in love I can be attracted to murder Avis to get her out of the way, although I'd not normally break the law even over a small matter.'

'That's stupidly wrong.'

'Can't you conceive special circumstances in which you'd commit a crime? To save your family, for instance?'

'That's not what I call a crime.'

'Not if what you do seriously hurts another family?'

'That's the kind of argument I hate,' she snapped.

'But it helps to explain why the detective is ready to believe I may have killed Avis.'

'You're beginning to frighten me. Until now I've just been furious that anyone could be so stupid as the detective: but you've really been saying that he can go on and on until . . .'

'Until he's convinced I killed Avis.'

'No one yet knows for certain that she's dead.'

'Every day during which there's no word from her makes it look more certain, doesn't it?'

.    .    .    .    .

Monday brought sharply contrasting weather. The wind veered round to the south, died away, then returned as a gentle breeze. There were few clouds in the sky and the bright sunshine brought colour to the land. It was an Indian summer, unexpected, probably brief, but very welcome.

Kelly left the supermarket, where he'd talked to the security officer, and waited for the traffic to ease before he crossed the high street. A heavy lorry growled past, belching exhaust, and this was followed by a second one, almost as large. He could remember when Ferington had been a small market town, lorries had been reasonably sized and any criminal who carried arms and used them was liable to be topped. Now Ferington was large, sprawling, and dirty, juggernauts were shaking foundations, and criminals were carrying guns on any major job and using them without second thoughts. Progress?

He crossed. The bank had a dignified, Queen Anne exterior, but inside it had been modernised with bullet-proof screens – again, progress? He went to 'Enquiries' and asked to have a word with the manager.

The manager was in his late middle age and he had the calm manner of someone who had lost all sight of ambition. 'Yes, I did read about Mrs Scott's car being found in the sea. Very sad. I've met Scott a couple of times. Seemed a nice man. . . . But you say you aren't certain about Mrs Scott?'

'We can't be certain she's dead just because her car went over the cliff and so until we find her body or the surrounding circumstances become overwhelming it has to remain a presumption. Which is why I'm here. I need to find out a few details about her account and wondered if you'd give them to me without me bothering over a court order?'

'What exactly are you asking for?'

'To know what kind of use she made of her account

before last Tuesday and whether any use of it has been made since then.'

'I'm prepared to give you general answers, but not specific ones.'

'Fair enough. And there's one thing more. Her husband told me she was left roughly thirty thousand pounds by her father – how much of that has she still got?'

The manager studied Kelly. 'So it wasn't an accident?'

'What makes you think that?'

'The movement of cash in her account would help to show whether she's still alive. The amount of her capital remaining can't have any relevance to that particular question.'

Kelly made no comment.

The manager pressed one of the buttons on the internal phone and asked someone to dial the computer for a read-out of the past month's movements of Mrs Avis Scott's account.

In a short time a young, smartly dressed woman brought in a strip of paper which she handed to the manager. He studied it. 'Up until the seventeenth there was considerable movement, in the order of about five withdrawals a week. There was one withdrawal on the seventeenth. Since then there has been no movement.' He crumpled up the paper and dropped it into the wastepaper basket by the side of the desk.

'And do you know off-hand the answer to my second question?'

'I doubt the capital is as great as it was: if pressed, I would describe her as inclined to imprudent extravagance. More than that, I am not prepared to say.'

Kelly thanked him and left.

.    .    .    .    .

Judith loved the country, but she did not have the hungry passion to own large tracts of it as did her husband. She looked down the sloping field, rough grass only because no tractor could work safely on it, to the low flat ground which was bordered by the bourn that ringed one of the woods and she enjoyed the scene without once bothering to think that all this was hers.

A Land-Rover, driven too fast, came bouncing along the flat land. Julian seemed always to be competing against somebody or something, she thought.

He saw her and turned, to come charging up the slope and then stop with squealing brakes. 'What's the matter? What's happened?' he shouted through the opened driving window.

'Why should anything be the matter?'

'When I saw you there, I thought . . .' He became silent.

What had he been afraid of? For days something had been deeply troubling him, but he wouldn't say what it was. 'The change in the weather made me come out to enjoy the sun while it lasts,' she said. She paused, but he made no comment. 'By the way, I've asked Kevin to come to supper.'

'You've what?'

'I've asked Kevin to supper. What's so odd about that? The poor man must be in a terrible state.'

'I told you I'm going over to see Michael to-night.'

'You said to-morrow night.'

'D'you think I don't know what I said? You'll have to entertain him on your own.'

'I really think that in the circumstances you should put Michael off.'

'Well, I don't. You ought to have checked with me

first.' He engaged first gear and drove on, again too fast for strict safety.

Why wouldn't he see Kevin? she wondered sadly. Sympathy never altered facts, but it could help to soften their impact. For her, some of the sunshine seemed suddenly to have gone from the scene.

．　　．　　．　　．　　．

Nothing of much importance was happening in the world, but to-morrow's papers had to be filled so minor stories, useful in such an emergency, were picked up, dusted, and used. Provincial journalists found that they were suddenly able to sell local stories to the nationals.

The phone rang.

'Evans here, *Ferington Gazette*. Can you tell me if you've had any news of your wife, Mr Scott?'

'I've heard nothing,' Scott replied. He replaced the receiver.

．　　．　　．　　．　　．

In his office, Craven yawned. 'Well?' he said, when the yawn was finally over.

'I'd say there's not a shadow of doubt she's dead,' replied Kelly, who sat in front of the desk. 'There's been no movement in her bank account for a week although before that she was always drawing money.'

'Where's the body?'

'If the tide took it well out to sea, the coastguards say there's every chance it won't come back ashore.'

'All right, let's accept that she's dead. Was she murdered, did she commit suicide, or did she die in an accident?'

'There's nothing to indicate suicide. Accident? Was

94

she too boozed to know what she was doing and in the car park engaged drive instead of reverse and was over the edge before she could react . . . I've been on to Traffic and they've estimated that, taking a starting point from ten feet behind the wooden railings, there was enough reaction time available, even allowing for the effect of drink, for the driver to comprehend what was happening and to panic brake. On top of that, the lights weren't switched on, a man was driving the car when it passed Polgate Wood, the driving door was probably sprung deliberately, the steering wheel was wiped down as was the bottle, there was a thread caught up in the driving door, and there were marks in the ground which could very readily have been made by someone's shoes . . . I'd say it was murder.'

'What was the motive and who was the murderer?'

'Avis Scott was worth a certain amount of capital and there's another woman. Scott isn't very successful in his writing: I talked to a bloke I know in a book-shop and he reckons Scott will be lucky to clear fifteen hundred a year. That won't keep any sort of a household going to-day.'

'The facts seem clear, but you sound doubtful?'

'Mrs Ballentyne swears there's never been any-thing between them and maybe I'm becoming soft, but I keep wanting to believe her.'

'What's this paragon of virtue like? A twenty-year-old blonde with a figure of fire?'

Kelly smiled briefly. 'She's homely, but fun.'

'Make your mind up. You don't get a woman who's both.' Craven yawned again. 'We're going to have to widen enquiries. And it's time to search his place. See a magistrate first thing to-morrow and swear out a search warrant.'

# 16

The car turned into the drive of Honey Cottage. 'It looks a bit of a lop-sided shack,' said Detective Constable Thompson.

Why couldn't Jim Thompson realise that much of the charm of the cottage lay in its twisted angles which spoke of past centuries? wondered Kelly. He parked in front of the garage and climbed out of the car. Thompson came round the bonnet: he was a large man in his early twenties with a very full face that became almost puffy around the lower cheeks: he had a bluff, cheerful manner, but there was often a challenge to this and he had a quick temper.

'Don't push him, he's not that kind of a bloke,' warned Kelly.

'I don't push anyone unless he tries to push me, Sarge. D'you say he writes books?'

'Yeah,' replied Kelly, as he reached into the back of the car to bring out a small, battered suitcase.

'There's a pansy job for you.'

Kelly led the way round to the porch. He knocked. As they waited the wind, a little stronger and perceptibly colder than the day before, plucked at their clothes.

Scott opened the outer door.

' 'Morning, Mr Scott. D'you mind if we come in to have a look around the house?'

'The answer to that is simple: yes, I do mind, very much.'

'I promise everything will be left exactly as we find it.'

'You'll leave everything, full stop. I subscribe to the old idea that a man's house is his castle.'

Thompson said belligerently: 'We've a warrant.'

As subtle as a seven pound hammer, thought Kelly annoyedly, as he led the way inside.

'May I see it?' demanded Scott.

Kelly handed him the warrant, folded into three with the embossed seal outwards. He skimmed through it. 'All right, I can't legally do a damn thing to stop you. What d'you expect to find: a skeleton in the cupboard?'

'It's happened,' said Thompson, before he appreciated the play on words. He flushed: he could not stand being made to look slow.

'Shall we start upstairs?' said Kelly.

Scott's anger gradually changed to interest as he watched them search, quickly but very methodically, the spare bedroom. When Kelly took a large torch out of the suitcase and switched it on, he said: 'What's that for?'

Kelly didn't answer until he was kneeling on the well worn carpet. 'Sometimes things which you wouldn't otherwise notice show up in a bright, oblique light.' He played the beam across the carpet. 'Like this, for instance.' He reached forward and picked up a pin which he handed to Scott. 'Apart from saving your feet if you walk around barefoot, that ought to ensure me good luck for the day.'

The detectives checked the floor, walls, the built-in cupboard in which hung a number of dresses, the old and battered chest-of-drawers, and the blanked-off fireplace, even to the extent of pulling away the front of the grate and looking through the dust which lay beneath the bars.

Kelly indicated the small work table on which stood a typewriter with a half-typed sheet of paper in the roller. 'Is that the latest coming along?'

'It is the latest, but right now it's more a case of going than coming.'

'I just don't know how you can sit down every day and write.'

'Nor do I, when the interruptions are almost constant.'

'Tell you what, Mr Scott, you'll be able to get your own back in your next book: introduce a couple of detectives who are absolute bastards.'

'I write fiction, not fact.'

Kelly laughed, but Thompson stared with belligerent dislike at Scott.

They went out to the small landing and Kelly looked up. 'I suppose that trap door's up to the loft? We'd better have a shufty up there later on. Jim, you can climb up when it's time, you're still young.'

They entered the second bedroom. 'I take it this is your bedroom? And you keep your clothes in that cupboard?' He crossed to the built-in cupboard and opened the doors. In addition to Avis's clothes, there were inside an elaborately embroidered dressing-gown, one suit, one sports jacket, and three pairs of men's trousers. 'Are these all your clothes, Mr Scott?'

'Yes.'

The sports jacket was a dark green and clearly the thread found on the door of the Jaguar had not been drawn from it. 'There's only the one sports coat here – don't you have at least one more, perhaps for gardening?'

'When I'm working, I wear a sweater. When I'm not

working, I wear a sweater.' Scott smiled, for the first time since the detectives had arrived. 'No tailor's ever become rich on my trade.'

It sounded true, thought Kelly, yet a coat was easily burned. But would a man who had thrown himself out of the Jaguar as it rushed towards the three hundred foot fall ever have realised that he might have snagged his jacket on the car door and that the police might become suspicious and a thread from the jacket would be important evidence? A man who could plot a book might well have the imagination to foresee events . . .

He picked up the four pairs of men's shoes in turn. The brown brogues had mud around their toe caps. 'We'll have to take these along with us.'

'What in the hell for?'

'To scrape out the mud for comparison tests.' He noticed that Scott's expression remained blank. 'We're looking for a pair of shoes which made certain marks on Stern Head.'

'Scrape away, but scratch the leather and I'll sue you for a new pair.'

Kelly put each shoe in a large plastic bag: he sealed the bags, tied on to one a card which noted the date, place, and time, and which he initialled.

They searched the chest-of-drawers, the bed-side tables: they unmade the bed and checked the mattress and base and then remade the bed: they rolled back the carpet and underfelt: they checked all surfaces by torchlight.

Downstairs, in the dining-room, Kelly studied the sideboard. 'That's a lovely piece of furniture.'

'It should be,' replied Scott, remembering what Avis had paid for it.

'When I was young I thought I'd become a cabinet

maker. Trouble was, they wanted me to work for nothing as an apprentice. Couldn't be managed because the family needed me to make a wage.' He ran his finger-tips lightly over the marquetry. 'I often wonder whether I'd have been any good. It would be something to think that in a couple of hundred years a piece of my furniture might come up in Sotheby's.'

'Who's worried about what happens in two hundred years?' said Thompson, who preferred white pine furniture.

'Us old 'uns, lad.' Kelly jerked his head in the direction of Thompson. 'These days they don't appreciate anything unless it's disposable.'

The relationship between himself and the detective sergeant defied an accurate description, thought Scott, since it was such a complicated mixture of friendliness and suspicion.

They went from the dining-room into the kitchen and then into the sitting-room. Kelly examined the two small bookcases on either side of the fireplace. 'You haven't any of your own books here?'

'No.' Scott didn't explain. Had his books been successful, they might have been there: as it was, he preferred to keep them well out of sight.

The floral patterned carpet ended four feet from the north and south walls and three feet from the east and west ones. The chairs and settee were set on the cork-tiled floor, just clear of the carpet.

Thompson picked up the cushions on the settee and then dropped them back in place, unintentionally making it obvious that he reckoned they were wasting their time. Kelly, making a mental note to blast him for his slackness, followed and reached down with his fingers between the sides of the settee and the fixed seat cushions. Half-way along the right-hand

side his fore-finger came into sharp, and momentarily painful, contact with something. By careful
manipulation, he brought into view a jade seahorse
necklace with a very fine gold chain. He studied it.
'That's beautiful! I suppose it's your wife's?'

Scott shook his head. 'It's not hers.'

'Are you sure?'

'Quite certain.'

'Might not your wife have bought it last Tuesday,
after you'd gone to London, which is why you don't
know anything about it?'

'I suppose so . . . But if she were going to buy a
piece of jewellery, I'm pretty certain she wouldn't
choose that.' Avis would never have enjoyed anything
so relatively unsophisticated.

Kelly remembered the withdrawal from her account
on the Tuesday – had the sum been large enough to
have bought this? The point would have to be checked.
'I think I'd better hang on to this for the moment,
Mr Scott. You'll have a receipt, of course.'

After placing the necklace in a plastic bag, he
knelt in the middle of the carpet, switched on the
torch, and swung the beam around. As it passed the
fireplace and approached the settee, two small spots
of irregular reflected light became visible.

He went over and shone the torch directly down-
wards: he could just make out two patches of what
looked like glossy varnish, greeny brown in colour.
Dried blood? 'We're going to have to lift a couple of
the cork tiles and send them off for checking.'

.    .    .    .    .

The detective constable turned off Oxford Street
and made his way to Chapman Road. He entered the

101

gaunt building and climbed the stairs to the third floor.

When Fiona Holloway opened the door his first impression was that she was a badly made-up man in drag. Her hair was bright ginger, her face over-long, her features masculine, her make-up crude: her body was thickset and powerful. But then she spoke and no man could have imitated her rich, musical voice.

The sitting-room was large but naturally gloomy and it was made gloomier by the many pot plants which all had large dark green, dusty leaves and reminded him of his great aunt who'd loved aspidistras.

They sat and he told her the reason for his visit and he saw, with embarrassment, tears well out of her large eyes.

'He's killed her,' she said, her voice choking.

'We can't yet even say for certain that Mrs Scott is dead, Miss Holloway.'

'I know she's dead.' The tears increased.

'You know Mrs Scott quite well, don't you?'

'She was my oldest friend.'

'Have you seen much of her recently – say in the past two years?'

'She . . . she often used to come and stay here.' She finally used a delicate, lace-edged handkerchief to wipe the tears from her puffy cheeks.

'When she stays here, does she talk much about herself?'

She nodded.

'Has she ever mentioned any men with whom she is friendly?'

'Why do you ask that?'

'Because we have to check the possibility that she

may be friendly with a man other than her husband and . . .'

'I've told you, Kevin killed her.'

The D.C. sighed.

'He hated her. All he wanted was the other woman.'

'Then you've no reason to believe she's friendly with any other man?'

She stared at him for a long time, then suddenly shouted: 'She told me, she's never ever looked at another man.'

.    .    .    .    .

A photo of Kevin Scott, together with a short biographical sketch, was on the back of the dust jacket of all his books and this proved good enough to be cut out and used for identification.

A D.C. questioned each member of the staff at Ferington Railway station: had he or she ever seen this person passing through the station and, if so, when was the last occasion? One ticket collector thought he'd seen the face before, but as to when that had been . . .

'No dice,' said the D.C. on his return to the station. He dropped the photo on to Kelly's desk. 'And the job's given me aching feet and a throat so bloody sore it feels like it's been swallowing razors.'

'You need a break. See that pile of forms over there? Take 'em off and type out fair copies in triplicate.'

'You just can't win,' said the D.C. philosophically.

.    .    .    .    .

Scott was making coffee when a boy of about four-

103

teen rode down to the garden gate, leaned his bicycle against the thorn hedge, and walked round the house a newspaper in his hand, whistling painfully out of tune. He left the paper in the porch.

Scott collected the paper but didn't begin to read it until he was seated at the dining-room table with toast, butter, marmalade, coffee, and a four-minute-egg in front of him. He had finished eating the egg and was half-way through his third piece of toast when he turned a page of the paper to see a photograph of Avis. He was shocked even though the telephone call of the previous day should have warned him that a further reference in the press was likely.

He read the article beneath the photograph. There was still no evidence of what had happened to Mrs Scott, despite extensive police enquiries. Her husband, Kevin Scott the well known author, confirmed that he did not know where his wife was and Mrs Ballentyne, a close friend, was also unable to help.

It was all there, for those who could read between the lines.

# 17

Sidney Walsh, the younger of the two receptionists at the Red Barn Motel, finished reading the sporting section of the daily paper and then, since he wasn't on duty until the evening and had nothing better to do, leafed through the other pages. A photograph of a woman caught his attention. She looked, he decided knowledgeably, a right good screw. He decided that something about her face reminded him of someone. He tried, but failed, to pin down the memory and then read that she was probably dead. He lost all interest in her.

.    .    .    .    .

Jane now wished she had refused Kevin's invitation to lunch. But he'd been so insistent and she'd been feeling depressed . . . Each time she met him she became increasingly aware of the growing affinity between them and this was something that she still believed she had to fight, though without really knowing why. After all, she could be quite certain that Steven would never have expected her to remain a grieving widow. Perhaps it was the knowledge that the degree of their friendship must rest on whether Avis were alive or dead and that seemed wholly macabre.

When she entered the small Italian restaurant, with the brightly coloured murals on the wall, she saw that he was seated at a corner table, by a window. He looked up, saw her, and smiled as he came to his feet, but she noticed that even if his mouth smiled, his eyes didn't.

They sat. 'How's the work going?' he asked.

'Much as usual, which means that everybody seems to hate everybody.'

'It's not like you to be so cynical.'

'If you'd seen the work I've been doing this morning, you wouldn't be surprised. Ridiculous little arguments enlarged into great big matters of principle: an ounce of common sense or give-and-take and everything would have blown over ages ago.'

'Fortunately for the legal profession, common sense is almost as rare as a spirit of give-and-take.'

'Now you're being cynical.'

'Then let's have a drink and both mend our ways.' He signalled to a waiter, who handed them two menus. They ordered drinks.

'Do you come here often enough to advise me on what's good?' she asked.

'Normally I only come here when I'm celebrating good news from the writing field. I can't remember the last occasion.'

'Have you ever thought of giving up your writing and turning to something else?'

'No, because it's all I've ever wanted to do.'

'If you're lucky enough to be doing what you really want to, you've got a head start on most people, so stop complaining.'

'Yes, m'am.'

She smiled. He put the paper down by his side on the chair. He had intended to show her the paragraph right away, but he wanted to see her go on smiling.

It was three-quarters of an hour later, over their second cup of coffee, when he placed the newspaper on the table. 'The nationals have picked up the story of Avis's disappearance.'

She spoke uncertainly. 'Does that matter so terribly? I mean, the local rag carried the news last week.'

'The *Gazette* stuck to the bare facts. The reporter who wrote this story obviously had a direct line to the police. He opened out the newspaper and folded it at the page in question.

She read quickly and her expression changed from one of worry to one of anger. She looked up. 'So now the whole world will think we're leaping into bed together.'

'I'm terribly sorry,' he said quietly.

Her voice became still sharper. 'We've got to do something. They can't print this sort of thing and get away with it.'

'They haven't directly coupled our names together. Even if we could demand and get some sort of published explanation, they'd probably manage to put one in that meets the law but makes everyone who reads it twice as convinced as before.'

'Are you suggesting we do nothing?'

'Yes.'

'Do you always lie down and let the world trample over you?'

'If that's the only sensible course to take.'

Her shoulders slumped. 'I'm talking stupidly. Qui s'excuse s'accuse. And in this day and age, who gives a damn about who's bedding who?'

'You, for one.'

She nodded miserably.

.  .  .  .  .

For the second time that day, Kelly rang the

insurance brokers whose name Scott had given him the day before.

'I've been through our records and Mrs Scott did not ask us to insure a jade seahorse necklace, as described by you.'

'But she's always insured the rest of her jewellery?'

'As far as I know. Obviously I can't answer for certain without checking what jewellery she possesses against the list of pieces insured.'

'I had this necklace valued and it was put at between five and six hundred. At that value, would you have expected her to insure it?'

'Certainly. One or two of the pieces insured are valued at only a couple of hundred, even to-day.'

Kelly rang off. The bank manager had, after judicious persuasion, again checked Avis Scott's account and he reported that no sum larger than twenty-five pounds had been drawn at any one time within the month preceding her death. If she had not bought the necklace, how had she come by it? A lover? There could be an explanation of why it had not been insured. But Fiona Holloway's evidence strongly negated this possibility. And how and why had it come to be tucked down the side of the settee?

.    .    .    .    .

The forensic laboratory telephoned at mid-day on Saturday, just as Craven was about to leave to return home, determined to enjoy his first half day off for nearly a fortnight.

The two spots on the cork tiles were of human blood, type AB. This was the rarest of the four basic types and was possessed by roughly three per cent of the white population. Because the blood was dried, it had been impossible to make further tests to determine the MN factor. The two spots had dropped from a low height – probably between 6 and 10 centimetres – as evidenced by their shape, in particular the lack of any outer 'bobbles' to the main section.

# 18

As Scott backed the hired car out of the garage, a Cortina turned off the road. Kelly stepped out on to the drive. 'I obviously only just got here in time,' he said breezily. He grinned. 'There's no need to panic, though: this time it's just a couple of questions and then I'll get from under your feet.'

'Don't you blokes ever take any time off?' Scott found it virtually impossible not to respond to the detective's cheerfulness.

'You sound like my wife a bit earlier on, although she became rather heated about things.' Kelly shrugged his shoulders. 'If there were ten days in the week, I guess that still wouldn't be enough.'

'If I suggested a coffee, would you say you were too busy?'

'Don't go to any bother,' said Kelly weakly.

Scott switched off the engine of his car, then led the way into the house. He made the coffee and carried it into the sitting-room.

Kelly helped himself to sugar and milk and stirred. 'We've had word through from our forensic laboratory on those two cork tiles we took away from here – remember them?'

'I'm hardly likely to have forgotten them, am I? Especially since I've had to put that rug over the gap to stop anyone tripping and falling.'

Kelly did not look at the rug but kept his gaze concentrated on Scott's face. 'Those two spots were dried human blood.'

'If that's so . . .' began Scott.

'You can accept it as fact.'

'Then I've not the slightest idea who it came from.'

'It fell from a height of between six and ten centimetres. If a person's standing and the blood drops from that sort of height, it's obviously come from around his ankles. If he's lying down, on the other hand, it could have come from almost any part of the body . . . Have you recently bled when you've been in this room?'

'No.'

'As far as you know, has your wife suffered any injury which could have caused the bleeding?'

'No.'

'What group is your blood?'

'I've a note of it upstairs.'

'And would you be able to tell me your wife's group?'

Scott went upstairs to their bedroom. He opened the top left-hand drawer of the chest-of-drawers and brought out the old diary in which both their blood groups, together with other personal information, were recorded.

He returned downstairs. 'I'm group O. My wife is AB.'

'Thanks,' said Kelly.

It had been impossible to discern from Kelly's expression whether the information had been of any particular significance. Scott said, conscious his voice sounded strained: 'Does that tell you anything definite?'

'Only that those two drops could not have come from you.'

'Did they come from my wife?'

**111**

'They might have done, but no one's ever going to be able to take it any further than that.'

.    .    .    .    .

Melville-Jones, assistant to the Director of Public Prosecutions, was tall and thin, pernickety in dress, and pedantic in manner. 'We have three initial points of major importance to consider. First, is she dead: second, if she is dead, how did she die: third if her death was criminal, who was responsible?'

Why, thought Craven, did lawyers so enjoy repeating the same thing time after time? The detective superintendent fidgeted with a matchstick and tried to work out his chances of getting back to county H.Q. within the next hour and a half. Kelly stared at the far wall.

'Is Mrs Scott dead? On the evidence available we may assume that she is dead, but yet may not presume that she is. I will deal with the point in some detail.

'When a person's car is known to have gone over a very high cliff to become a total wreck, then clearly – unless the driver is known to have got clear before the crash – it is reasonable to assume he, or she, was in it. That assumption is weakened when the car is recovered, but no body is found inside it. A sprung door offers a reasonable explanation for the absence of the body but cannot by itself strengthen the now weakened assumption.

'If Mrs Scott is alive she will need money. Her account is dormant, but if her disappearance was deliberate, we have to consider the possibility that she has a further source of money not known to us. Friends have heard nothing from her, friends who obviously would have expected to hear were she alive...'

It was ten minutes before Melville-Jones finally said: 'So, gentlemen, we can say that at the moment we may not presume that she is dead: but in time this presumption will arise even if no more evidence comes to light provided there is no indication, however slight, that she is still alive.'

'How long?' asked Craven bluntly.

Melville-Jones tapped his finger-tips together. 'Very, very difficult to give a clear-cut answer. But should a further three months pass with the position unaltered I would probably hold that sufficient time had passed.

'Now, let us move on to consider the evidence in the light of a presumption that Mrs Scott is dead. Did she, perhaps while under the influence of drink, drive over the cliff accidentally? Or was she murdered and the car driven over the cliff to make is seem like an accident?

'If it was an accident, then she must have driven the car to Stern Head. Yet we have the evidence of Jenkins that her car was on the road at about nine o'clock on that Tuesday evening being driven by a man. Jenkins is a man of dubious character, but more importantly, how certainly can an observer at night, looking through the rear window, identify the driver of a car as a man or a woman? We are living in a time when even in broad daylight it is sometimes difficult to differentiate between the sexes . . .' He suddenly chuckled, surprising the three detectives, especially Kelly who had been dozing.

It was almost mid-day before Melville-Jones finally began to collect together his papers. 'So there we are, gentlemen. Time must pass before death can be presumed. And unless further evidence comes to hand, then a charge of murder against the husband will not lie.'

# 19

Jane went into Reynolds's office and put four letters on his desk. 'Could I have a word with you?'

'Of course,' he answered. 'Grab a chair and tell me what's bothering you.'

She sat and folded her hands on her lap. 'I suppose you've read in the papers about Mrs Scott's car having gone over Stern Head?'

'Yes.'

'And that . . .' She sat a little straighter. 'And how my name was mentioned along with Kevin Scott's?'

He nodded.

'It's horrible that papers can print that sort of innuendo. I said we ought to make the paper retract it, but Kevin insists it's much better to leave well alone. Is he right?'

'Libel by inference is the very devil to prove and if you start gunning for a newspaper they so often manage to get their own back. So my advice would be, grin and bear it.'

'It seems so weak to do nothing . . .' Her expression slowly changed from indignation to worry. 'There's something else I wanted to ask. In law, can someone be charged with murder if there's no body?'

'They can and have been. It's one of the common legal fallacies that there can only be a trial for murder when there's a corpse. If the surrounding circumstances go to show overwhelmingly that someone has died at the hands of an identified person, but the

114

body has not been recovered, then that person will be charged with murder.'

'But what if he doesn't know anything about her death?'

'Then the surrounding circumstances aren't going to show overwhelmingly that he murdered her.'

'But if they do,' she persisted.

He spoke very carefully. 'There's an old legal aphorism to the effect that witnesses can lie, but facts cannot.'

'Yet the interpretation of those facts can be a lie?'

'Of course.'

'Then an innocent man could be charged with murder?'

'He could.'

'But the trial must prove his innocence?'

'There is reason for believing that in the past innocent people have been tried and found guilty of murder. They most certainly have been of lesser crimes.'

'I've always thought . . . I've always believed that in this country our law couldn't make that kind of ghastly mistake.'

'It's about as just as any law can be, but it's not perfect. Or to qualify that, because it's in the hands of humans, its administration isn't perfect.'

She felt very frightened.

.    .    .    .    .

For his thirteenth birthday, Mike Grierson was given a metal detector and on Saturday, a dreary day with dirt-washed clouds blanketing the sky, he told his mother he was off to find a fortune in Park Wood. She said to be back by a quarter to one, in time to wash for lunch.

115

Park Wood had once belonged to the priory – now a ruin – and it was said that in the time of Henry VIII the prior, determined to save their treasure from the state's confiscation, ordered this to be hidden in the woods. Both the prior and the monks who had buried the treasure were subsequently murdered and so no-one knew in which part of the woods the treasure had been buried . . .

Mike's enthusiasm survived half a dozen soft drink cans and fourteen cartridge cases, but became noticeably weaker when, within ten feet of the road, he spent over three minutes digging up a fifteenth cartridge case. He sat down on a tree stump and reflected that a hundred and fifty acres was really rather a lot of land.

After a long rest he reluctantly resumed his search and eleven paces on, as he went round a large clump of brambles, the detector's note changed once more. He dug, finding the soil surprisingly loose but initially seeing no significance in this.

The spade met something solid. He knelt and began very carefully to clear the earth away. Soon, he uncovered a hand, on one finger of which was a large costume jewellery ring.

    ·     ·     ·     ·     ·

The body was sketched and photographed. Then four P.C.s, wearing green overalls, rubber gloves, and wellingtons, eased a canvas sheet underneath and lifted it out. More photos were taken, the pathologist made a preliminary examination, and the body was cocooned in thick plastic bags and carried out to the road where it was put in the back of an undertaker's van which drove the five miles to the nearest mortuary.

Later, at the mortuary, a detective constable viewed the body. He wrote out a detailed physical description and a list of the clothes and jewellery, now in a number of plastic bags. A précis of the physical description was sent to all divisional police stations and to the central index of missing persons.

. . . . .

Kelly studied the report, newly received over Telex. There seemed little doubt the body was that of Avis Scott. He looked at a map. Park Wood, near Lower Melford, was four miles from the main road. The murderer had buried her on his way back to London . . .

He spoke over the phone to the detective inspector in Lower Melford. 'We've just had your message in, sir, and it looks like we can put a name to the corpse: Mrs Avis Scott, last seen on the seventeenth of July.'

'The date fits with the pathologist's estimate of the time of death.'

'Would you give me a run-down on the clothes and any jewellery? If it still looks right after I've checked with the husband, I'll bring him up for an identification.'

The call completed, he went down to the courtyard and finding the C.I.D. car was for once available drove off in that.

He spoke to Scott in the low beamed sitting-room of Honey Cottage. 'I'm sorry to say we've had word that a body has been discovered in a wood near Lower Melford and there's reason to believe this may be the body of your wife.' Scott was shocked but showed none of the signs of panic which might have been expected. 'Can you remember the clothes your wife was wearing on the Tuesday?'

Scott stared at the fireplace. 'I think she was in a blouse and pink slacks,' he finally said.

The dead woman had been wearing a skirt, a blouse missing a button, a slip with a torn strap, and pants. 'What were her marriage and engagement rings like?'

'The wedding ring was chased platinum, her engagement ring was opal, set around with small diamonds.'

Kelly now had no doubts left about the identity of the dead woman. 'I'm afraid you'll have to come to the mortuary with me to see if you can identify the deceased.'

He swallowed heavily. 'I can't.' He saw Kelly's expression. 'All right, suppose it was you – how in the hell would you like to have to go to a mortuary to see if you could identify the body of your wife after she'd been buried in some woods?'

'I'd detest it, but I'd go because that would be the only way in which I could be certain.' He moved towards the door. 'Is there anyone you'd like to ask to come along with you?'

Scott shook his head.

    .     .     .     .     .

Scott watched as the white-coated attendant slid one of the large drawers out of the refrigerated cabinet. He wasn't as sickly frightened as he had expected, but his right hand was suffering quick spasms of shaking.

'Would you just stand over here, please,' said the attendant, in a matter-of-fact voice. He pulled the white cover back a couple of feet.

Scott stared at the face he had last seen that Tuesday morning: he remembered the day he'd proposed to her when he'd promised that soon his name would be a household word: he remembered her mother telling him that she was a very good cook, omitting to mention that she knew nothing about budget cooking . . .

'Is she your wife?' asked Kelly.

He nodded.

The attendant replaced the white cover and slid the drawer back.

.     .     .     .     .

Scott climbed out of the car. Kelly said: 'Good night, Mr Scott.'

He walked down to the gate, helped by the car's headlights since it was now dark, and round to the porch. He switched on a light and only then did the car back, turn and leave.

Even though in the end he had not loved her, he knew a terrible, icy emptiness because he had loved her in the beginning. He crossed to the corner cupboard and picked up the telephone receiver and dialled. As soon as the connexion was made, he said: 'Talk to me for a while. Blame me for interrupting your favourite telly programme, but talk.'

'My God, what's happened?' asked Jane.

'I'm just back from the mortuary at Lower Melford. Avis's body was found buried in some woods and I had to go and identify it.'

'Where are you?'

'The detective brought me back home after the traditional double whisky.'

'Why didn't you come here? At a time like this, to go back to an empty house! Have you still got the car you've been hiring?'

'Yes.'

'Then get in it and drive straight over.'

# 20

The pathologist handed the very small knife to his assistant. He looked over the tops of his half-moon glasses at the exhibits officer, who was talking in an undertone to the coroner's officer. 'That's it, then,' he said.

He walked over to the double sink and peeled off his gloves, dropping them into a paper sack. His assistant undid the tapes of his green overalls and helped him out of them. He pulled off the wellingtons with the aid of a boot-jack and slipped on his comfortable, worn, brown casuals. 'Death was caused by the functional event known as vagal inhibition. There are some asphyxial changes, but only of a trivial nature. It is possible that someone took a grip on her neck, wanting to keep her quiet, and she died very suddenly, indeed almost instantaneously: there may well have been no intention to kill. It is a death which prostitutes unfortunately suffer from time to time.'

. . . . .

Melville-Jones took a handkerchief from his pocket and brushed his lips with it. 'The assailant may have intended to strangle her, or he may have intended merely to quieten her. In this latter case. the offence was manslaughter unless he tried to quieten her in furtherance of rape, when it becomes murder. A husband cannot legally rape his wife, therefore he cannot legally be guilty of attempting such rape. But as a matter of some interest – and not in connexion with this case – a person may be found guilty of an attempt of a crime which is, in fact, impossible.'

Craven's expression said plainly that the law could be, and often was, more than an ass.

'There is historical logic for this,' said Melville-Jones.

'Of course, sir,' replied Craven smoothly. The law was rich in historical absurdities.

'There is one very important question we now have to consider. Where did Mrs Scott die?' He looked at the detective superintendent, at Kelly, and finally at Craven. 'You claim she died in the sitting-room of Honey Cottage. But although the blood on the two cork tiles can be shown to be of the same group as hers, and although this group is common to only a very small proportion of the population, you cannot prove that the blood was hers. But let us assume that you could. Could you then go on to prove it had been shed in the course of her death and not at some other time?'

'No, sir,' said Craven. 'But when all the evidence is studied it must surely become overwhelmingly probable that we're right.'

'In a court of law, Inspector, the difference between overwhelmingly probable and provably certain is, as I would have thought you understood, of vital significance.'

The chief superintendent nodded. Kelly, seeing Craven was looking in his direction, winked.

'Now let us consider the question of motive. Your contention is that the motive for the murder (correct me if I'm wrong, but I don't believe you have considered to any great extent the possibility of manslaughter) was twofold: Scott wanted his wife out of the way because of his friendship with Mrs Ballentyne and he wanted his wife's money. Where is your proof that his friendship with Mrs Ballentyne goes beyond the bounds of decorum?'

What a way of putting it! thought Craven. 'That sort of proof is very difficult to come by, sir.'

'Every time you have questioned either the lady or Scott, each has consistently denied that their friendship is more than platonic.'

'Miss Holloway was told by Mrs Scott . . .'

'What the deceased told Miss Holloway is not proof.'

'But it indicates – '

'Proof, Inspector!'

'All right, sir,' said Craven doggedly ,'if the motive for the murder – or manslaughter – wasn't what I've suggested, what was it? All our enquiries have failed to turn up so much as a hint of any other reason for someone wanting her dead. The evidence is that Mrs Scott was not having an affair, she was not – '

Melville-Jones sighed. 'The negative approach again. Inspector, it is the prosecution, not the defence, on whom the burden of proof rests.'

The detective superintendent spoke heavily. 'There isn't the evidence to bring a case, is there?'

'No,' answered Melville-Jones curtly. He collected up his papers and began to pack them in his brief-case.

.    .    .    .    .

Craven brought two pints of bitter over to the corner table in the pub. He sat. 'Damnation to all lawyers.'

'I'll drink to that,' Kelly said, as he raised his glass. 'What did the big white chief say afterwards?'

122

'He moaned, of course, but not for more than a quarter of an hour. He hasn't been at H.Q. quite long enough to have forgotten that sometimes a case just won't come right.'

'I suppose the case will now have to go into cold storage?'

Craven drank deeply, wiped his mouth with the back of his hand, and put the tumbler down on the table. 'When I started as a rosy cheeked P.C., who thought right and wrong were two very different things, and we had a murder case we worked at it until we reached the end, even if that took months. But these days, unless it's unusually horrific or the victim's important, we go for so long and then we have to give up because of pressure of work – though eventually we'd crack it.'

Craven had never learned to come to terms with failure, even when the cause of such failure lay outside his control, Kelly thought.

'I wonder what sort of a life our kids will know when they're our age? A complete breakdown of law and order?'

Kelly drank. While a man could enjoy a pint and a fag, things couldn't really be that bad.

# 21

Powell walked along the dirt road towards the cow kennels which stood on a large raft of concrete. One of the farm hands was cleaning the slurry. Powell climbed the earth bank of the lagoon. His father had taught him one thing which he had never forgotten: good farming needed muck. Fertilise one field of grass with artificials and another with dung for five years and note which grew the better grass.

He stared past the edge of a copse of chestnut, due to be felled soon, at part of the herd of Friesians, four fields away. When they'd bought Tregarth House the cattle had had to be taken off the land in most years by the beginning of October because of the lack of enough drainage: now even after considerable rain they stayed out until November. Every extra week on grass meant more profit.

There had been once or twice when he'd decided that if Kevin were charged with the murder of Avis he would have to go to the police and tell them what had really happened. But each time he had had only to step on to the land and feel it springing to his weight, to look at the herd and the sheep, to know that he could never tell the police the truth because to do so would be to risk losing everything.

It had very nearly been disastrous for him. But then he'd been a bloody fool. When a man had to choose between a woman and land, he shouldn't need to hesitate.

.    .    .    .    .

When the high-rise divisional H.Q. first came into view, beyond the council car-park, Jane stopped. But almost immediately, she resumed walking. She had to act because she could no longer stand seeing Kevin worry himself sick.

In the front room, the duty sergeant was talking to an elderly, harassed looking man and a P.C., who was plainly finding it an onerous task, was typing.

The P.C. stopped and came up to the counter. He noted her wedding ring. 'Can I help you, madam?'

'I'd like to speak to either Mr Craven or Mr Kelly, please.'

'I'll check who's in. Would you give me your name, please?'

She sat on one of the bench seats and picked up a magazine from the nearest low table. She leafed through this, not bothering to read anything more than the captions under some of the photographs.

The P.C. lifted the end flap of the counter and crossed to where she sat. 'I've spoken to Sergeant Kelly, Mrs Ballentyne. He'll be along very soon.'

Some ten mintes later, Kelly came through a door-way to the right of the counter and as he approached, she thought how tired he looked. ' 'Morning, Mrs Ballentyne.'

'I need to have a word with you,' she said quickly.

'Then let's go to one of the interview rooms: we won't be disturbed there.'

He led the way along a corridor and immediately before the corner pushed open a door for her to enter a room. It was small, with one barred window, painted a light green and white: the only furniture was a table and four chairs. On one wall was a framed list of printed regulations in eye-squinting type.

The moment she was seated, she said: 'I've come to –'

'Would you hang on a moment? A colleague, Detective Constable Thompson, is joining us.'

As if on cue, there was a quick knock on the door and Thompson entered. Kelly introduced him. He brought out a notebook and put this on the table.

She spoke calmly. 'I've been lying to you about Kevin and me: we've been lovers for some time. My husband was dead and Kevin and his wife didn't get on, so it just seemed . . . The reason I've always denied everything is because I've felt kind of guilty as my husband died not so very long ago. Also, we didn't want Avis to have the chance to make it appear that the break up of the marriage was entirely Kevin's responsibility.' She paused, then said with more force: 'On the night Avis died, Kevin was with me at my flat.'

'Mrs Ballentyne . . .' Kelly stopped. Had he been on his own, he would have risked warning her that she could only cause harm by inventing an alibi, but since Thompson was present he dare not do this.

'Kevin used to tell Avis he had to go up to London to see his publisher and he'd be staying the night at a friend's flat. He would go up to London, but then he'd get an early train back to Ferington and walk to my flat and wait there for me to return from work. The next day he'd stay until just before the time he'd told Avis to pick him up and then he'd go to the station and join all the people coming off the train.'

'Is this what happened on the seventeenth and eighteenth of last month?'

'He was with me all night and didn't leave the flat until about five the next afternoon to be at the station when the four eighteen from London arrived.'

'Did anyone visit your flat during the Tuesday evening?'

'Nobody did, no.'

'Is there anyone who can verify the fact that Mr Scott was with you?'

'I've told you that he was. There was no one else around.'

'Is there anything more you'd like us to know?'

'There's nothing more to know.'

'Then your statement will by typed out and I'll ask you to sign it if you agree that what's written is what you've just told us.'

'You've got to understand that he was with me from five in the evening until five the next day.'

'Didn't you go to work on the Wednesday?'

She tried to hide her consternation. 'I . . . I rang the office up and said I had a cold.'

'Thanks for coming and telling us, Mrs Ballentyne. We won't keep you long before the statement's ready for signing.' He nodded at Thompson who stood and left.

.  .  .  .  .

Craven hurried along the passage and into his office. Kelly entered. 'We've had a visitor, sir.'

'Give me all the bad news at once and make me feel lousy.'

'Mrs Ballentyne came here to admit that she's been lying. She and Scott have been having it off for some time and on the Tuesday he went up to London but didn't stay and returned to be at her flat by five. He was there until about five on the Wednesday, when he walked to the station and joined the crowd coming off the four-eighteen from London.'

'Witnesses?'

'They stayed at her flat the whole time and saw no one. She's admitting everything now to prove he couldn't have had anything to do with his wife's death.'

'By God!' exclaimed Craven. 'Just when we'd decided we had to give up! Now we've got the motive all cut and dried. Not even that smart bastard from the D.P.P.'s office can knock that.'

# 22

Jane faced Scott in the hall of Honey Cottage. Nervousness made her sound defiant. 'I've just been to the police station. I told them I've been lying all this time and that we are having an affair and that you were with me all Tuesday evening and night.'

'Why?' he asked hoarsely.

'I couldn't stand seeing you worrying yourself ill because people were stupid enough to think you could kill your wife. I was a fool not to have done it before – the world's been convinced we're lovers from the word go.'

'But why in God's name didn't you come and talk it over first?'

'You'd have tried to argue me out of it . . . You know, Kevin, we've learned a lot about each other.'

'But not yet enough,' he said. 'Jane, ring your boss and tell him you can't return to the office to-day. If he wants a reason, tell him you've broken a leg. You've proved yourself a good liar, so he'll believe you.'

.     .     .     .     .

Feeling as if he had been walking for hours, Kelly limped into the station courtyard. A dog handler, about to climb into the cab of his van, called across: 'Skipper, your old man's been shouting for you. Twice through the parade room wanting to know where in the hell you'd got to.'

Kelly continued into the building, careful to favour his right foot. On the door of the lift shaft there was a small printed notice saying that the lift was out of order. Cursing high-rise buildings, he slowly limped his way up the flights of stairs to Craven's room.

'Where have you been?' demanded Craven.

'Trying to find a bloke called Walker in order to get a witness statement.'

'That doesn't take all afternoon.'

'It does if someone's pinched the C.I.D. car and you have to walk and everywhere you go he's just left.'

'You ought to send a D.C. out on a job like that.'

'I would have done if you hadn't got hold of them all first.'

Craven suddenly grinned. 'You look like you've been having a rough time.'

'It wasn't too bad after everything went numb.' Kelly sat down and lifted his right leg to rest his ankle on his left knee.

'I've been thinking about the Scott case,' said Craven.

Kelly pulled off the shoe and rolled down the sock. He stared resentfully at the well-formed blister.

'The truth has to be facing us, if only we've got the wit to recognise it.'

Kelly prodded the centre of the blister.

'The first D.I. I served with was a great man for maxims. One of his favourites was, "If a case becomes all glued up, look for the illogical." D'you follow.'

'Not really,' replied Kelly. He wondered if it were true that one ran a grave risk of septicaemia if one pricked a blister?

'If something's illogical, the odds are it's important. So what's illogical in this case? Remember telling me something was puzzling you?'

Kelly looked up, a vague expression on his face.

130

'You couldn't understand where the seahorse neck-lace had come from. Scott swore he'd never seen it before and his wife hadn't drawn the money to buy it, she hadn't insured it although she'd insured pieces of jewellery of much less value.' Craven leaned forward in the chair and rested his elbows on the desk. 'How certain were you that Scott was telling the truth when he said he'd never seen the necklace before?'

'As certain as I could be when I'd no proof one way or the other.'

'Let's accept you were right. So what was she doing with jewellery he hadn't seen before?'

'Someone gave it to her.' Kelly rubbed the skin around the blister. 'Only we dug and dug and there hasn't been so much as the hint of a boy friend. Miss Holloway swears there wasn't one.'

'Never mind – we chase up the illogical.'

Kelly sighed. 'I suppose you want me to question everyone again?'

'First off, I want you to get the press to print a photo of that necklace. Spin 'em a story which get's 'em interested. Someone may come forward and give us the history.'

Kelly slowly pulled the sock up over his sore foot.

. . . . . .

As far as the national press was concerned there was now more than enough material to hand and so a five-week-old murder case involving a housewife was out. But the *Ferington Gazette*, perhaps due to a temporary lack of local corruption, was short of copy and so they printed the photograph of the neck-lace together with an accompanying story.

. . . . . .

131

Judith did a great deal of charitable work, partly because she liked helping people, partly because this enabled her to come to terms with her own wealth. On Thursday mornings she attended the weekly meeting of the local Red Cross committee and on the afternoon of the penultimate Thursday of each month she chaired a meeting of the management committee of the Rayman Community. When she had the two meetings in the one day, she usually had lunch in Ferington at the White Swan, an old coaching inn.

She was in a corner table and after the waitress had taken her order she picked up the local paper and looked through it. On page eight there was a photograph of the necklace which had been found by the body of Avis. The photograph had not reproduced at all well but it did remind her that neither Julian nor she had heard from Werner and Hall who'd said some weeks ago that they hoped to be buying in a fine jade seahorse necklace. She made a mental note to get Julian to ring them to find out what had happened to it.

After lunch there was still an hour and a half before the committee meeting was due to begin and she decided to walk down to the public library. Her route took her down through the car park in which was a public call-box. It was empty and she suddenly decided to ring Werner and Hall herself to save Julian the bother. She spoke to Mr Leach. 'I've been wondering if you ever bought in that seahorse necklace you told me about?'

'Yes, indeed, Mrs Powell. A piece of considerable quality. But surely . . .' He paused. 'Have you not seen it?'

'Of course not. How could I have done?'

He coughed. 'May I ask, is it your birthday soon?'

132

'What on earth are you talking about?'

'Well, it seems . . . Mrs Powell, your husband came in some time ago and bought the necklace. Obviously, it's been kept back as a surprise for you.' He burbled on about how the style of the carving suggested the piece came from the Langchung area . . .

She thanked him and rang off. Julian wouldn't be keeping the necklace as a surprise. First of all, he never remembered anniversaries and secondly whenever he bought her a piece of jade he handed it over as quickly as possible and with thinly veiled resentment: one piece of jade could easily represent half a dozen top quality Friesians, sired by premium bulls . . . No. He'd bought it and returned home and she'd been out and he'd forgotten all about it.

# 23

The committee meeting of the Rayman Community had been a tiring one. By the end of it she had a headache and when she drove into the garage at Tregarth House this headache had become severe.

Powell was watching television and the sound was turned so high that it made her head throb more violently. She adjusted the volume control.

'I can't hear it now,' he complained bad temperedly.

'It's perfectly loud enough,' she answered, for once speaking sharply. 'I've had a heavy day, Julian, and I've a beast of a headache.'

'You shouldn't waste your time with all those ridiculous committee meetings.'

Yet again, she wondered sadly why he could not feel more sympathy for others. 'Did Olive leave supper out before she went off?'

'It's a rat's tail of a meal.'

'You know she's always in a hurry to get away when it's her night off . . .' She stopped. He'd once milked cows three times a day for two years without one single break. Perhaps he was entitled to be intolerant. 'I had lunch at the White Swan. They've put the price up twenty-five pence.'

'Everything goes up but the prices at the farm gate.'

'That reminds me, I bought a copy of the local and in it there's a photograph of a jade seahorse necklace which was found near poor Avis. I remembered Werner and Hall were supposed to be buying in a necklace like that and as I'd some time after lunch I rang up Mr Leach to ask him what had happened to it. He said he sold it to you some time ago . . .' She stopped abruptly, shocked by the expression on his face. 'Julian, what's the matter?'

He struggled to regain some measure of self-control. 'Are you ill?'

'Can't you ever stop bloody fussing?' he shouted, fright panicking him.

'I . . . I was just trying . . . I'm going up to bed. I don't want any supper.'

She waited, expecting at least a few words of commiseration, but he said nothing, merely staring at her with an expression which could easily be interpreted as dislike. Very close to tears, she left.

He poured himself out a strong brandy and soda. After all this time! When it had seemed certain all danger must be past. He desperately tried to convince himself that she would not realise the two necklaces had to be one and the same: that her fierce sense of loyalty would prevent her coming to the logical conclusion. But sooner or later she must wonder and when that happened . . . She'd understand he had betrayed their marriage and, in betraying it, had mocked it . . . Loyal and loving, knowledge of the betrayal would make her hate, as emotionally as she had loved.

He poured himself another brandy. How to avoid catastrophe? He tried to concentrate his mind, yet all he could do was to think in quick snatches of panic. Then, suddenly he remembered Reginald.

He hurried through to the library. The phone here was a separate line and so there was no chance of Judith's picking up the bedroom extension and overhearing him. He dialled. A woman answered.

'Is Reginald there?' he asked.

'Who?'

135

'Isn't that Reginald Powell's house?'

'You want Reg? Blimey, you had me confused.' She laughed coarsely.

He waited, breathless now from tension and fear.

'Who is it?' demanded Reginald Powell.

'It's Julian here ...'

'You dumb bastard! Didn't I tell you not to get in touch with me?'

'Something terrible's happened.' In a rush of words, he told his brother about the necklace. 'The moment she realises it has to be the same necklace, she'll know Avis and I ...'

'Your old woman doesn't understand anything at all yet?'

'Not yet. But when she ...'

'Where is she now?'

'Up in bed. She came back from Ferington with a bad headache ...'

'Who else is in the house with you?'

'No one. It's the housekeeper's night off.'

'All right. So I'll come and see you and we'll talk it over. Listen, don't go and tell anyone I'm coming along.'

'Of course I won't.'

'You're bleeding dumb enough . . . I'll be there around ten. Leave the doors unlocked.'

'You'll think of something, won't you?'

'Likely.'

.    .    .    .    .

Reginald Powell and Anderson left the car, stolen just before leaving London, half-way up the drive and walked to the house. Powell was in the downstairs sitting-room: he wasn't drunk, but neither was he

136

sober. It was a simple job to batter him to death with lead-filled coshes.

Because the death of Avis Scott had proved how easy it was to make fools of the police, they now set the scene to make it seem as if there had been a burglary and Powell had interrupted it and in consequence had been killed.

# 24

Kelly stared at the chalked outline on the parquet floor: by the roughly outlined head was an irregular patch of congealed blood. On the face of things, there was little doubt about what had happened, but there were inconsistencies. Take the time of death. The police doctor had given this, subject to all the usual qualifications, as having been between ten and midnight. Yet mobs who specialised in country houses worked the early hours of the morning, for obvious reasons. Take the strong-room. From appearances, it dated back to when the house had been built. Any twirler expert would be inside it within five minutes and any mob working country houses would take along a twirler expert, but a D.C. had checked the three locks with an illuminated probe and no attempt had been made to force them. Had the intruders killed Powell, panicked, and fled? But professional mobs seldom panicked. Had it, then, been not an experienced country house mob but a bunch of tearaways? Yet the window of one of the French doors had been expertly smashed after coating the glass with an adhesive and covering this with mutton cloth: the closed circuit alarm had been cross-contacted: Powell's injuries, designed to kill, had been expertly inflicted . . .

An experienced detective learned to gain a feel about a case and right now he felt there was something wrong about this one. He looked through the shattered French window and watched a line of uniform P.C.s searching the garden.

A man, dressed in a dark suit, entered the sitting-room. 'I've done all I can so I'll be on my way. I've told the housekeeper to get in touch with me if necessary, but as I've sedated Mrs Powell quite heavily there shouldn't be any trouble.'

Kelly said: 'I need a quick word with her.'

'She's much better left alone.'

'It is very important.'

'You'll not get any sense out of her.'

'But if I'm brief, will it do her any harm?'

'I suppose not,' replied the doctor reluctantly. 'But five minutes at the very most.' He left.

Kelly went into the hall and up the stairs with their elaborately shaped balusters. As he reached the landing, around which were pots in which grew indoor plants, a D.C. came along the passage on his left. The D.C. reported that all the rooms except Mrs Powell's had now been searched and nothing of the slightest significance had been found. Kelly asked him which was her room.

There were two beds, set against a single quilted headboard, with matching tables on their outsides. The drawn curtains were a rich burgundy velvet, the large carpet a Persian kaleidoscope of reds, blues, and blacks: there were two matched serpentine-fronted chests-of-drawers, beautifully and elaborately inlaid, which immediately, if briefly, drew his attention: on one of the walls hung a painting of sunflowers, orgiastically coloured, which he guessed was a van Gogh.

She lay in the right-hand bed with the small table lamp switched on. Normally plain, shock and grief had coarsened her features. Her eyes held the luminosity which came from repeated tempests of weeping.

He said how sorry he was and the genuineness of his sympathy was obvious. 'I need to know one or

139

two things as soon as possible if we're to catch whoever broke into this house last night. . . . The housekeeper says you were out most of the day – when
did you get back and when did you last see your
husband?'

She continue to stare at him.

'Mrs Powell, have you any idea what the time was
when you got back here?'

'I had a headache,' she murmured. 'And he was so
angry.'

'Your husband was angry?'

'All I did was phone them. How could I know?'

'How could you know what?'

'That he'd bought the seahorse necklace from the
jeweller's.' She began to moan, low, choking sounds.
Kelly left.

He returned downstairs and went along the main
corridor, past a door still lined with green baize, to
the housekeeper's small but cosy sitting-room, con-
verted from one of the pantries.

Olive Bins, middle aged, had the features of someone who had often been battered by life but who had
always fought back. She said in her deep voice, in
answer to the first question: 'I spent the night with
my sister in Ferington and didn't return until just
before nine this morning. The police were already
here.'

'Will you think back carefully and then tell me
something? Has anything happened recently which in
the light of Mr Powell's death makes you now think
that it might be significant? The kind of thing I'm looking for is someone who's tried to be friendly and has
asked about the routine of the house, telephone calls
which were cut off the moment you answered them,

parked cars which could have been spying out the lie of the land.'

She shook her head. 'No, there's been nothing like that.' He brought a pack of cigarettes from his pocket and offered it. She shook her head, but said she'd no objection to his smoking. 'You told one of my blokes that Mrs Powell has some sort of collection which is kept in the strong-room and you thought that maybe that was what the men were after – what kind of a collection is it?'

'It's jade. There's quite a lot of it and I've always understood it's pretty valuable.'

'Is there any chance you know the name of the jeweller's Mrs Powell usually went to?'

'Not off-hand. But she has a small book of telephone numbers she uses quite often and I'm sure it'll be in there – maybe I could work out which it is.'

.        .        .        .        .

Craven stood near the telephone as Kelly spoke to Leach of Werner and Hall and there was an expression of irritation on his lean, sharp face because he couldn't make out the course of the conversation.

Kelly finally replaced the receiver. 'Powell bought a jade seahorse necklace from them at the beginning of September for six hundred quid. He was able to describe it fairly well, but says that if we'll get our necklace to him he'll be able to make a positive identi-fication.'

'How does his description fit?'

'Well enough.'

'Then since I don't believe in coincidences a mile high, it is the same. Which surely means there has to be a connexion between this murder and Mrs Scott's.' He walked over to the nearest window and stared out at the view. Until now, such a possibility hadn't arisen. Since it had, all the facts had to be re-evaluated. Kelly's hunch was probably right. The prime reason for the break-in the previous night had been murder, not theft: for some reason, Powell had had to be silenced. Craven swung round. 'First thing is to get over to Scott's place.'

.    .    .    .    .

Craven deliberately presented the news in the baldest terms as soon as he and Kelly were in Honey Cottage. 'I suppose you've heard already that Powell was murdered last night?'

Scott, standing close to the bottom of the stairs, stared at him with an expression of surprise which could hardly have been simulated.

'D'you mind telling me where you were last night?'

'Are you trying to say I murdered him as well?'

'I'm saying nothing of the sort. But in view of what's already happened, I have to put the question.'

'There's a link between the two murders?'

'It's possible.'

Scott spoke pugnaciously. 'I was with Mrs Ballentyne from five-thirty until sometime after one. And this time there are enough witnesses to back up Ananias and us.'

Craven said nothing.

'We went to dinner at that new Mexican restaurant which has just opened outside Hemscross. Given half an encouragement one of the waiters sings love songs to the ladies and we stayed on until they shut at almost one. I tipped far more than I can afford, so I hope they'll remember us.'

Craven nodded.

.    .    .    .    .

On Saturday afternoon, when the day had become dull and limp and the overcast sky was glooming for rain, Mrs Bins showed Craven and Kelly into the upstairs sitting-room at Tregarth House.

Judith was seated on one of the bench window seats of this very large, sparsely furnished room, staring out past the balcony with its graceful wrought-iron rails at the scene her husband had so loved. She wore black and it was ironic that this colour suited her tall figure and austerely plain, heavy face.

Two comfortable chairs had been placed near the bench seat: between them was a small occasional table on which was an ash-tray and a lacquer box, opened and half full of cigarettes. They sat.

'You want to ask me some questions?' Judith said.

'We need your help if we are to identify the man or men who broke into this house on Thursday night,' replied Craven.

She was a quiet woman who could too easily be hurt vicariously by another's misery, but for her husband's murderers she knew only a violent hatred. Normally a woman of personal secrecy, she now withheld nothing. She relived in detail memories which a person of a different and less honest character must have tried to conceal, even from herself.

When Craven and Kelly left her, sitting very upright by the window, they both had the uncomfortable feeling that they had been present not only at an interview but also at a confession.

## 25

Craven's room at divisional H.Q. was thick with smoke. Craven, unusually smoking a pipe, pointed the stem at Kelly. 'All right, we're building with bricks which may be all straw: but they're the only bricks we've got right now.'

'Just so long as they don't all collapse at the same time.'

'You always were a pessimistic bastard,' he said, in a rare moment of friendly joshing. He put the pipe down on his desk. 'I don't think we're too far wrong.'

Kelly didn't think so either, but life had taught him that it was fatal to become too certain.

'Powell gave that necklace to Avis Scott and then he became scared his wife would hear what he'd done. That left him out on a limb because the estate was in her name and she's the kind of woman who if she learned he was using someone else's bed would have kicked him right out. I suppose he might have claimed his half, under a reverse women's lib, but that would have made him look a Charlie and he obviously hadn't any sense of humour. He had to neutralise Avis Scott and the best way of doing that was to arrange to have the necklace nicked because if she no longer had it to prove the truth, he reckoned he could convince his wife she was lying.

'One or more men went to Honey Cottage to nick the necklace when Scott was in London. In the course of the robbery, which failed because they never thought to search the settee, she died very suddenly.

They phoned Powell to tell him what had happened and it was that call which shattered him to such an extent that his wife still remembers it so clearly.

An attempt was made to make the death look like suicide or accident, but this failed. On the facts available to us then, we had a case of murder against the husband, but there just wasn't sufficient evidence to charge him.

'Then we had our lucky break. Mrs Ballentyne became so desperate to take the pressure off Scott – not realising that, ironically, we'd decided to put the case into cold storage and so it was already off – that she tried to fake an alibi for him. Because of this, we got a photo of the necklace printed and because of that Powell was caught in the jaws of a nutcracker. What he didn't have the sense to realise was that now he'd have to be murdered to save the skins of whoever had killed Mrs Scott.

'Having said all that, how are we doing now? I'll tell you. We're doing badly. We don't know who Powell had been in contact with over Mrs Scott. When he was murdered there was no one in the house but his wife and she was laid out with a headache. There's not a meaningful dab and not a useful trace. We've sent word through to the grassers and you'd think they'd all taken vows of silence . . .'

Kelly said slowly: 'Powell was at home the night the attempt was made to nick the necklace, so he hired someone. Assuming it's the same someone who killed him, we're dealing with professionals. Where would a man like Powell find himself a villain?'

Craven stared at him for several seconds. 'You know, there are times when you begin to earn your keep! If he'd asked around casually, every grasser in the area would have heard about it.'

145

'So it has to be someone he knew. How does a farmer come to know a villain?'

.    .    .    .    .

Kelly and a D.C. from the local division arrived at Maude Bowring's house at eleven fifteen on Sunday morning. Kelly, showing quiet, warm sympathy, spoke generally to her until some of her nervousness had subsided, then he said: 'We thought you might be able to help us, Mrs Bowring. What we're trying to do is draw up a list of all your brother's relatives and friends.'

'But I can't really help you. You see, he never had much to do with us. Used to send a card at Christmas – or rather Judith did – but that was all. And so we don't know none of his friends.'

'Did you see him very often?'

'Hardly ever. Leaving out the last time, I don't suppose we'd seen him in nigh on ten years.'

'When was the last time?'

'It must've been a couple of months back,' she said vaguely. 'And then, of course, he didn't come to see us: not really.'

'Not?'

'He wanted to find out how to get hold of Reg. That's one of my other brothers.'

'Had he lost all contact, then?'

'He . . . He never understood that it wasn't really Reg's fault.' She blushed from shame.

'Fault over what, Mrs Bowring?'

'That . . . that he'd been to prison,' she murmured.

.    .    .    .    .

Craven and Kelly drove up to London on Monday morning, arriving at the divisional H.Q. at ten-twenty.

The divisional D.I. spoke to them in his room.

'We've pin-pointed Powell for you. He's living in a house in Vermont Street. We've had nothing on him recently.' He pulled a sheet of paper forward. 'After your phone call, I sent word out to one or two grassers to see if they could turn up anything. There's not much come in, except that Powell's been seen around recently with a bloke called Anderson: Jock or Snout Anderson. Is the name of any significance?'

'None,' answered Craven. 'But the odds must be that if it's Powell we're after he had help.' He thought for a moment, then added: 'I'd like to take 'em both at the same time – d'you think we could work two teams?'

'Easily done.'

.      .      .      .      .

Kelly and a local D.C. had driven to the drab, side-by-side house in which Anderson was living. Shocked to learn the reason for their visit, he had not been panicked. Adopting a sullen, dully stupid attitude – an easy task – he blocked all their questions with the same primitive air of ignorance.

Kelly, his good humour apparently undented even by Anderson's manner, said: 'You've been working with Reg.'

Anderson lumbered over to the fireplace. The front room hadn't been cleaned in days because his common-law wife was a slattern: there were several empty beer bottles in the uncleared grate, cigarette stubs had overflowed an ash-tray, paper lay scrumpled up by the side of an empty bookcase, and on top of the television set was a plate on which were the congealed remains of a meal. 'Don't know no Reg.'

147

'I've told you,' said the D.C. wearily, 'you two have been seen together.'

'Don't know no Reg.'

Kelly, seated on a battered arm-chair, spoke earnestly. 'Wise up, Snout. Reg is real smart so when he understood which way things were going, he started making certain he was all right even if that dropped you head first in ten feet of mud. He told us he'd said to leave the woman alone, but you got wild and killed her, even though you didn't mean to.'

This was sufficiently near the truth for Anderson momentarily to fear that he had been double-crossed.

The detectives waited. Anderson picked up a pack of cigarettes from the mantelpiece, found it was empty, screwed it up and threw it into the grate.

'Don't let him send you down for a lifer,' said Kelly. 'The truth is, isn't it, he killed her?'

'Get stuffed.'

The D.C. sighed. 'You try to help 'em, but they're too dumb to be helped.'

'Let's talk about Reg's brother,' said Kelly. 'Lived in a big house, lots of silver and jewellery and the place wide open. I suppose Reg called it an easy mark?'

Anderson walked back to the window, the panes of which were covered with dirt.

'But it turned out that the real job was to croak the brother. Reg was sure taking you for a sucker.'

There was another short silence.

'Snout, I'm giving you just one more chance because I'm soft enough always to feel sorry for the sucker. We're about to search this place and find proof you've been out on both the jobs. If you don't speak up, those nick doors are going to shut behind you for more years than you can think about. But speak up now, tell us how Reg lied and tricked you, and we'll do what we can for you.'

Anderson cursed them.

'All right,' said Kelly, 'let's start looking.'

'Where's your warrant?'

'Do you mind?' said the D.C. scornfully.

They searched slowly and carefully, but by the time they reached the last room in the small house, a bedroom in the same state of slatternly disorder as everywhere else, they had found nothing of the slightest consequence. It had perhaps, thought Kelly wearily as he went into the bedroom, been stupid to hope they'd find some of the silver from Tregarth House, but Powell and Anderson must have thought themselves completely in the clear and in these circumstances villains often boastfully took the risk of keeping around them the proof of their success.

Anderson and the woman – her hair was in curlers, her dress was stained and torn – stood in the doorway and watched as Kelly began to search the bed and the D.C. the clothes cupboard. The woman in a shrill, penetrating voice kept asking Anderson what it was all about and he, in his hoarse, harsh voice kept telling her to belt up.

Having finished with the bed, Kelly let the mattress fold back into position and tidied up the bedclothes, even though they had originally been in disarray. He crossed to the single chest-of-drawers. Each drawer was a jumble of clothes, some of them dirty. The floorboards had on them only a small slip carpet and it was easy to make certain that there was no hiding place beneath them: the ceiling was cracked, with a chunk of plaster having fallen away in one place, but again a visual search was sufficient to be certain there was no hiding place above it.

The D.C. shut the cupboard door. 'It's clear,' he said.

So that was that, thought Kelly. And yet the evidence pointed to Reginald Powell and Anderson and beneath that air of brutish stupidity he was convinced there was the watchful tension of a guilty man . . .

'We'd best be moving,' said the D.C. He was in a hurry to get back to H.Q.

'I'm telling you, if you don't push off smart I'll bleeding well throw you out,' Anderson shouted, with the belligerence of a bully who, after a moment of doubt, once more felt himself to be in control of the situation.

As Kelly stared at him, he remembered something.

'Are you getting?' Anderson balled his fists.

'Cool it, Snout,' said the D.C. with bored authority. He spoke to Kelly. 'I've a job back at the station . . .'

'One last thing,' interrupted Kelly. He walked over to the wardrobe.

'I've checked there,' said the D.C., his voice expressing irritation.

Kelly pulled open the two battered doors. Some clothes were hanging up, others were lying in the bottom in untidy heaps: amongst those hanging was a check sports coat, in Harris tweed, reddish brown in colour. He lifted the hanger off the rail.

'What are you up to?' demanded Anderson, his belligerence now tinged with concern.

'Were you wearing this when you drove the Jaguar through the fence and over the edge of Stern Head and nearly left things too late for yourself?'

'I ain't . . .'

'I don't suppose anyone's told you that a length of thread from the coat was caught up on an edge of the door of the Jaguar? The lab's holding it for comparison tests.' Kelly smiled.

# 26

Over the phone, the editor said in his rich, plummy voice: 'I thought you'd like to know that your latest book has recorded some very satisfactory sales just when we were thinking of remaindering it.'

'*Mirabile dictu*,' said Scott. 'What's suddenly breathed fresh life into the dying?' He became hesitant. 'D'you reckon it's my slight change in style which has gone down with the public?'

'No, I don't think it was that.'

'Then was it the couple of good reviews I got?'

The editor coughed. 'As a matter of fact, Kevin, our travellers report back that the sales are up because you've been in the news. A little . . . outside publicity often helps, you know.'

Scott thanked the editor for phoning him. After replacing the receiver, he thought how he must have sounded ridiculous when he had assumed that it had been the quality of his work which had increased sales . . . Bitterness gave way to amusement. Life was a banana skin.

At that moment Kelly walked past the window, his mackintosh ballooning in the wind. Scott went through to the porch. 'As the actress said to the bishop in one of the intervals, this seems to be becoming a habit.'

Kelly stepped inside. 'A habit you'll be glad to hear is ending. I've just come to say that we've identified and arrested the two men who were responsible for the deaths of your wife and Mr Powell. I don't know

151

whether it will help at all, but there was no intention to kill your wife.'

He didn't know either. He had not loved Avis at the time of her death, but her death had hurt and a small part of that hurt had surely been the thought of men deliberately killing her.

'I'm very sorry for everything that's happened, but we had to do our job. I can only assure you that we tried to do it as fairly as possible. Now, except for the formalities, you won't be bothered by us again. You'll be able to give all your time to your books.'

But how to ensure that their sales remained up?

.    .    .    .    .

Jane was waiting outside her flat, her expression very worried. 'Kevin, has something terrible happened?'

He took hold of her, kissed her, and then led her inside and shut the front door. 'The police have discovered who killed Avis and Julian.'

'Oh, my God!' Her mouth trembled and she began to cry.

'Hold it. How can I propose to a woman who's acting as if this is the most miserable moment of her life?'

'You could try,' she answered, in a choked voice.